Sherlock Holmes
and the
Adler Papers

By the same author

The Travels of Sherlock Holmes
Sherlock Holmes and the Telephone Murder Mystery
Sherlock Holmes and the Boulevard Assassin
Sherlock Holmes and the Disgraced Inspector
Sherlock Holmes and the Hammerford Will
Sherlock Holmes and the Abbey School Mystery

Special Commission

Sherlock Holmes
and the
Adler Papers

John Hall

**BREESE
BOOKS
LONDON**

First published in 2001 by
Breese Books Ltd
164 Kensington Park Road, London W11 2ER, England

© Martin Breese, London, 2001

ISBN: 0 947533 591

Typeset in 11½/14pt Caslon by
Ann Buchan (Typesetters), Middlesex
Printed in the United States of America

Dramatis Personae

- Mr Sherlock Holmes, a famous consulting detective
- Dr John H Watson, MD, Mr Holmes's friend and associate
- Mrs Irene Norton, née Adler, an old acquaintance of Mr Holmes
- Mr Godfrey Norton, her husband
- Wilhelm Gottsreich Sigismond von Ormstein, King of Bohemia
- Karl-Heinz Siebald, also called Karl von Ormstein, the king's illegitimate half-brother
- Gottfried Baldur von Ormstein, Duke of Essen-Württemburg, the king's cousin
- Maurice von Ormstein, a young soldier and a distant cousin of the king
- Colonel-Baron Bertram von Gratz, a friend of the king
- Captain Markus, a young officer in von Gratz's regiment
- & Sundry landladies, hoteliers, cab drivers, loungers and buxom wenches

A Word to the Reader

When Dr Watson wrote of the 'King of Bohemia', he caused more problems than he realized. Attempts by Sherlockians to identify a real counterpart to the king have, without exception, failed miserably. Largely this is because by the time Watson wrote his tale the old independent kingdom of Bohemia had become an integral part of Austria-Hungary, and all the possible candidates for the kingship have their movements well documented. If Watson used 'Bohemia' in order to hide the real geographical location, and that seems the only possibility that makes sense, then it was surely because he had not the wit to invent 'Ruritania'. (Although his friend and medical colleague, Dr Conan Doyle, named a fictional ocean liner after that country.)

For all the integration, the Bohemians were not entirely happy with their Austrian partners, and resisted attempts to 'Germanize' the language, place names, etc, insisting on retaining Czech. (The Hungarians were similarly unhappy with the new order, and not at all upset when Austria-Hungary split into its component parts.)

For the purposes of this book, then, 'Bohemia' still has its independence, it remains a middle European kingdom which never joined forces with Austria-Hungary; the royal house of von Ormstein sits on the Bohemian throne; and the boundaries and street plans of neighbouring countries and towns have been liberally re-drawn where necessary. . .

A Word to the Reader

ONE

I have already told of how I lost touch with Mr Sherlock Holmes for a short time following my marriage to the former Miss Mary Morstan in the latter part of the year 1887. And I have recounted the dramatic way in which we renewed our acquaintance in March, 1888. It was then that Holmes was retained by the King of Bohemia to recover a compromising photograph from the adventuress Irene Adler. In a strictly limited sense, Holmes may be said to have failed in his mission because the photograph was never recovered, but the king was satisfied that the former Miss Adler, who had by that time married one Godfrey Norton, would never make the photograph public; and the king esteemed – and rewarded – Holmes highly as a consequence.

The acquaintance, once resumed, did not quickly lapse a second time. I accompanied, and I venture to think that I assisted, Holmes as he worked on various problems over the next few months. Towards the end of 1888 my own practice was rather busy – there were, I recall, a good many cases of influenza and similar complaints that winter – and I was perforce obliged to neglect Holmes to some degree for a time. However, by late February in 1889 my own list was less pressing than it had been for some time, and one bright but chilly day, as my travels happened to take me via Baker Street, I took the liberty of calling upon Holmes.

I was admitted by Mrs Hudson, and immediately noticed

a somewhat worried look on her face. 'It's Mr Holmes, Doctor,' she confided almost before I had stepped inside the door.

'Not ill, is he?'

'Not to say ill, no, Doctor. But he hasn't eaten this past two days.'

'Ahah!' I knew the symptoms well. Holmes evidently had some knotty problem in hand, and this was his way of resolving it, starving his body to clarify his brain. Medically preposterous, of course, but it would take a braver man than I am to persuade Holmes of that! I told Mrs Hudson, 'Pray do not concern yourself too much. I shall have a word with him,' and I saw myself up to the old familiar door.

I was sufficiently sure of my welcome to enter without knocking. As I had expected, Holmes was curled up in a chair by the window, smoking an ancient and foul pipe, and staring at a sheet of paper or something of the sort which lay on his knee. The window, I might add, was closed, so that the atmosphere was somewhat stuffy. 'Holmes?'

When he did not answer, I strolled over to another window and opened it, to let some air in. Then I went over to Holmes, intrigued to know what it was that so held his attention. I was slightly taken aback to see that it was nothing other than the cabinet-sized photograph of Irene Norton, née Adler, which Holmes had acquired at the end of the strange case of the King of Bohemia. 'Fine looking woman, Holmes,' I ventured.

Again, he did not answer me. 'Bright day, Holmes. Good day for a stroll. You must need a little fresh air by now. Prevent total collapse of your lungs, you know.'

He said nothing, but merely continued to stare at the photograph. I am, I make so bold as to say, the most mild mannered of men; and yet I admit that I was a touch nettled to be thus ignored. And for what? For a photograph of a woman who, when all was said and done, had been no better than she ought to be, and who was now married to a lawyer to boot! I have often remarked upon Holmes's powerful intellect, his rising superior to the ordinary feelings and fancies of humanity, his machine-like powers of reasoning; and yet here he was staring at a woman's picture like any moonstruck youth who feels Cupid's darts for the first time!

Very well, thought I, sitting down opposite him. 'Interesting case the other day, Holmes. Fellow was in the park – bright day, same as this – after luncheon at his club. Good lunch, too, with a bottle of something or the other. Beaune, I dare say. Anyway, he felt a touch sleepy, and sat down on a bench. He dozed off, started to dream he was in France, during the Terror. Caused by the Beaune, I expect. Imagined he was an aristocrat, trussed up like a Christmas goose, and handed up on to the guillotine. Well, the blade was wound up, and he heard a click as it was released, and a "whoosh" as it came down. Now, it chanced that his good lady happened to be strolling in the park that afternoon as well, and as she walked past his bench, she noticed him asleep there. Feeling that it wasn't the proper thing, she tried to wake him by tapping the back of his neck. Fellow thought it was the blade of the guillotine, and the shock killed him! Died of a heart attack without ever waking up. Curious, don't you think?'

I stood up, went over to the coal scuttle, and selected one of Holmes's cigars, the most expensive brand that I could find among the assortment in there, a fine firm cigar with a dark wrapper and a grand aroma, a cigar in the new shape with a taper at only one end that was just then replacing the old *figurado*. I cut the end leisurely, lit the cigar carefully, and watched the smoke curl upwards to the heavens.

Slowly, slowly, infinitely slowly as it seemed, Holmes turned his head towards me. 'If this fellow died without ever waking up, then how the devil –'

'Does anyone know what he was dreaming? That's the point of the story, Holmes. Rather good, don't you think? Heard it in the club last week.'

He laughed in his own silent fashion. 'Well, at least it got my attention, Watson.' He stood up and shook my hand, running an eye over me. 'You have been rather busy of late, I see. The influenza, I suppose? And you have not been entirely immune from the illness yourself, that is obvious. But now, happily, you are fit and well, and have even ventured so far as to make a short visit to Brighton within the last two weeks, staying, as I judge, not longer than the one night.'

Years of Holmes have made me immune; I did not rise to the bait. 'Right in every respect, Holmes. I won't ask how you knew.'

'Oh,' said he, a touch disappointed. 'Well, of course it is always a pleasure to see you, Doctor. I believe you made some remarks to me earlier, which I failed to catch?'

I nodded at the photograph, which he had put down on the table. 'I presumed to remark that the former Miss Adler was a good-looking woman, Holmes.'

'Was she?'

It was my turn to laugh. 'You certainly seemed to think so, for you were gazing at her likeness intently enough!'

'And you thought that it was admiration?'

'Perfectly natural, Holmes. Good-looking woman, middle-aged bachelor. And you yourself have expressed some sentiments of regard towards the lady, I think?'

He considered. 'From a purely professional point of view, Watson, I assure you.'

'Oh? And what did Miss Adler do that was so clever, then? She revealed the hiding place which you sought almost at once, as the result of a very simple deception. And then, when she knew you had been engaged on the case, she ran away to the Continent! Hardly a brilliant strategy, Holmes.'

It was Holmes's turn to be nettled. 'To the casual observer, perhaps not. But it stung, Watson, to be thus outwitted, and by a member of what I had previously regarded as the weaker sex. I have not often been bested; three or four men have done the trick, but only one woman. I have to admire Mrs Norton, as she now is.'

'H'mm. But you were so very intent when I came in just now, Holmes. And Mrs Hudson says you have been abstracted for a day or so? Surely there is more to this than a professional regard for an old adversary?'

'Your powers of deduction are happily unimpaired by a year of marriage, Doctor.' Holmes strolled to the mantel shelf and rummaged among the litter that covered its surface. He found a letter, and threw it across to me. 'That arrived two days past. Read it, if you would.'

I read: 'My dear Mr Holmes – You will, I am sure, recall the curious way in which I made your acquaintance almost a year ago. I have been out of England, as you know, since then, but now circumstances oblige me both to return to London, and to ask if I might consult you upon a professional matter. It will, I assure you, in no way compromise any loyalty you may feel towards His Majesty the King of

Bohemia, and it will, I venture to think, intrigue your sense of the curious. We were adversaries once, but when you have heard my story I think you will agree that we must work together now. With your permission, I shall call upon you today, at three o'clock. Yours sincerely, Irene Norton, née Adler.' I put the note down. 'Curious, indeed.' I glanced at the superscription. 'The Northumberland Hotel eh? And dated two days past, I see. Well, Holmes? I suppose you have heard the lady's story, and been ruminating upon it ever since? Don't just sit there, man! What did Miss Adler – or Mrs Norton, as I should say – want to see you about?'

He shook his head, and was silent for a moment. 'There you have me, Watson,' he said at last. 'The matter stands thus: as you observed, that note arrived two days ago, at eleven in the morning. I was as intrigued as you are, and wondered what it might be that had caused Mrs Norton to consult her old adversary in a professional capacity, as she put it. I was therefore waiting eagerly when three o'clock came, and went. At four, I grew restless, and at half past I sent a messenger to the Northumberland Hotel. He was back almost at once, and told me that Mrs Norton had left at half past two, and not returned! I went to the hotel myself, and got the same tale. Yesterday I sent again, twice, to find that Mrs Norton had not been back at all. And similarly, she had not returned this morning.'

'Missing two days from the time, then, that she set off to see you? Suspicious, that, Holmes.'

He nodded. 'There are two likely explanations.' He cocked his head on one side, and looked at me.

'One, that she got cold feet, thought better of consulting you, and ran for it. And, two –' and I broke off.

Holmes nodded again, but said nothing.

'Was her bill paid?'

'It was not.'

'Suggesting that the first possibility is not a probability?' I said. 'For if she had merely decided against consulting you, there was still no reason why she should not settle her account and leave all in order before catching the boat, or whatever she had in mind.'

'I concur. Which is rather disturbing.'

'It is indeed. It rather suggests that the second possibility, that Mrs Norton was prevented from seeing you by some person or persons unknown, and for no good purpose, is the correct one.'

'What would your course of action be, Doctor?'

I thought. 'I think I should go to the hotel again, settle Mrs Norton's bill, and ask that her luggage be sent here. And leave a message to that effect. Force her hand, so to speak. If she does return, and wants her bits and pieces, then she'll be obliged to come and see you after all!'

'Excellent!' Holmes leaped to his feet, and sought his hat and stick. 'Can you accompany me?'

'Nothing I'd like better.' And a few moments later we were out in the street, headed south.

A brisk walk soon brought us to the Northumberland Hotel. Holmes strode inside and approached the clerk, explaining that he had been asked to settle Mrs Norton's bill, and asking that her luggage be sent to 221B Baker Street as soon as convenient. The clerk at first demurred, but the name of 'Sherlock Holmes' did the trick. When the clerk left to see about the luggage, Holmes scribbled a short note, explaining matters to Mrs Norton, and he left that with the clerk, with the request that it be handed to Mrs Norton in the event of her return to the hotel, 'lest,' as

Holmes put it, 'there should be any small misunderstanding.'

'A wise precaution,' I said, as we left the reception desk.

'Oh, it is somewhat high-handed, I agree, but what else could we reasonably do? In all events, Mrs Norton will not continue running up her bill when she is not even occupying her room!' Holmes stopped as we reached the main entrance, and nodded to the uniformed doorman.

'Sir?'

Holmes produced the cabinet photograph of Mrs Norton that he had evidently concealed, unseen by me, in his pocket. 'This lady has, I believe, been staying here?'

The doorman looked at the picture with obvious appreciation. 'Yes, indeed, sir.'

'Did you perhaps see her leave the hotel two days past? Around half past two in the afternoon?'

'Now you mention it, sir, I did.'

'And did she perhaps ask you to call a cab?'

The doorman shook his head. 'I did ask, sir, but she glanced at her little watch – it was on a brooch affair pinned to her dress, you know – then asked me the time, as folks do even when they've just looked at their own watches, and when I told her, "It's half past two, madam", she smiled and said she had plenty of time, and she would walk.'

'H'mm. Thank you,' said Holmes, reaching in his pocket.

'Only she didn't.'

'What's that?'

'Begging your pardon, sir, but she didn't walk, the lady. She set off, fair enough, heading back the way I just seen you come, ten minutes since. But at the corner there,' he nodded to a spot no great distance away, near the corner of Trafalgar Square, 'a carriage pulls up, and someone inside calls out to her.'

'Man or woman?' asked Holmes at once.

The doorman shook his head. 'A man I think, sir, but I couldn't rightly see.'

'Carriage, you say? Not a cab?'

'A carriage, sir. Anyway, the lady looks up, and smiles, says a few words, nods her head and what have you. Then he – I mean, whoever was inside the carriage – says something more, and then the lady hesitates, so to speak, then she climbs into the carriage.'

'You didn't see a man, or anyone, step down to assist her?'

'No, sir. Not that the lady looked as if she would need any assistance, begging your pardon, sir. Very self-contained, as you might say. Determined.'

'Yes, indeed.' Holmes took a coin from his pocket. 'Thank you.'

'You didn't by any chance see any coat of arms, or anything of that kind, on the carriage?' I asked.

Holmes nodded approval, but the doorman said, 'Nothing of that sort, sir. It was just a hired carriage, you know. In fact, I almost thought I recognized the driver.' And he paused, significantly as it seemed to me, and glanced down the street.

Holmes at once put his hand in his pocket once more, but the doorman quickly said, 'No need for that, sir! Here, Bill!' he called, addressing a roughly dressed man who was propping up the wall a few yards off, the sort of lounger who hopes to make a few pence by opening cab doors for the gentry, and what have you, round about a large hotel. 'Bill, you know that carriage driver, thickset bloke, thinning on top, with a little scar over one eye? What's his name again?'

The lounger approached, eyeing Holmes and myself speculatively. 'Oh, I know. Tommy something, Tommy

Maunby, that's it. Works for old – that is, for Mr White. White's cab yard, sir,' he added to Holmes, 'down by the Embankment.'

Holmes took a second coin out, and threw it to the lounger. 'I am much obliged, sir. Come along, Watson.'

He led the way down Northumberland Avenue and turned under the railway arches near Hungerford Bridge, stopping at a high wooden gate which bore a roughly made hand-lettered sign, 'Whites Yard No Trepsassers', with not a vestige of punctuation and scant regard for spelling. A large middle-aged man with an alert expression walked up to us. 'And what can I do for you gents?'

'Mr White?' said Holmes, and when the man nodded, Holmes continued, 'I believe you have a driver named Thomas Maunby in your employ?'

'Tommy? I do, sir. Here, he's not in no trouble, is he?' asked Mr White.

'No, no. On the contrary, sir. My name is Sherlock Holmes, and I have reason to suppose that Mr Maunby may be able to help me with an investigation which I have in hand.'

Mr White made some appropriately incoherent remark as to the improbability of Mr Sherlock Holmes seeking out his – Mr White's – place of business for the purpose stated, and the great honour it conferred upon him, Mr White, and then went off to find his driver. He returned a very short while later, bringing with him that 'thickset bloke, thinning on top, with a little scar over one eye,' whom the doorman at the Northumberland Hotel had so accurately described. 'Here he is, sir,' Mr White told Holmes.

'Mr Maunby? I dare say Mr White has explained matters to you,' said Holmes. 'I wish merely to ask whether you recall a customer who hired you and your carriage the day before yesterday? The time I am particularly interested in would be around half past two.'

It was Mr White who answered. 'He paid for the whole day, sir. About nine o'clock in the morning, he came here. That right, Tommy?'

'Right enough, sir.' Mr Maunby grinned. 'Paid for the whole day, but I got finished early.'

'You say "he" paid,' said Holmes. 'The customer was a man, then? Did you know him, or get his name? Can you describe him?'

Mr White frowned. 'Can't recall as he gave a name, sir, and I certainly never saw him before. And now you mention it, he was well wrapped up, cloak and hat and scarf, so I can't say as I saw his face neither. Tommy?'

'Can't say as I did, sir. Nondescript, as you might say. And wrapped up, like Mr White here says.'

'H'mm. Well, then, he hired you and the carriage at nine. What then?'

'Well, sir, he asks me to drive round the corner and stop! Naturally enough, I asks him, is this as far as you want to go, sir? He just grunts, says "I'll tell you when to move", or words to that effect. Well, he'd paid in advance, I knew that, so I wasn't bothered, I just thought he was – well, an odd one, as you gents would say. Then, early afternoon, he wakes up, so to speak, says, "There's a lady there I wish to speak to, driver. Move on, and stop when I say". So I moves on a few yards, no more, and he calls to me to stop. Then he speaks to the lady.'

Holmes produced the photograph of Irene Norton once again. 'Was this the lady?'

Like the doorman at the Northumberland Hotel, Mr Maunby smiled appreciatively. 'It was, sir.'

'And did you catch anything of what passed between them?'

'It's this way, sir,' said Mr Maunby. 'This job, if you took notice, you'd learn all sorts of secrets. A bit like a doctor or a lawyer – or a private detective! Begging your pardon, sir. So you gets into the habit of taking no notice, as it were. Truth to tell, I was thinking about my dinner, having not eaten since breakfast, and as I recall, I was kicking myself, in a manner of speaking, for not nipping down and getting something to eat whilst the old – the gentleman, that is – was asleep, or not taking any particular notice of anything, as it were.'

'"Old", you say?' asked Holmes quickly. 'Was he old, then?'

'No, sir. Sorry, sir, just a manner of speaking. He kept his voice low, like, so I couldn't rightly say how old he might have been. No older than you gents, I dare say.'

'So you heard nothing?'

'I don't say that, sir. I just say that I couldn't repeat it word for word. But he asks her where she's going, something of the kind, and she says something like, "None of your business". Only –' he hesitated.

'Yes?' prompted Holmes.

'Well, sir, you're a man of the world. You know as well as I do myself that this business about "None of your business" can be said in a few different ways. What I mean is, a bloke can say it to you in the pub in a way that means he wants you to make it your business in the sense of wanting you to take a swing at him; but then a girl can say it to a bloke in such a way as it means that she wants him to make it his business in another way altogether, if you follow me, sir?'

'Indeed I do. And how did this lady say it?'

'Oh, easily enough, sir, on the face of it, and a dainty little laugh to go with it. But it seemed to me that she meant it, if you understand me.'

Holmes frowned. 'She tried to make light of it, but could not quite hide her concern?'

'You have it, sir! Anyway, he says something more, but – like I said – he kept his voice low, so I couldn't rightly hear him. Then the lady says, "I'll take some convincing", or maybe, "You'll need to convince me", or it might have been, "You'll have to go some to convince me", or anyway it was something on those lines. And he says, "Very well, if you'll give me the chance, I'll undertake to do that", as it might be. Something like that. And she hesitates a bit, then climbs into the carriage, and he tells me the address.'

'Ah! And what was the address?'

'It was number eighteen, Little William Mews, sir. In Mayfair.'

'And you took them there?'

Mr Maunby nodded. 'They got down, and the gent he says, "Thank you, driver, that will be all", and he hands me a half-sovereign over and above the day's hire that he'd already paid! So I comes back here, leaves the carriage, and goes off to find some grub.'

'And this number eighteen, Little William Mews? What sort of house was it? Anyone else there that you noticed?'

'It was a mews cottage and stable, sir, just as the name says. The stables each side was busy enough, but number eighteen was all quiet. I'd been through that way a week ago,' Mr Maunby went on, 'and there was an agent's board, "To Let", outside the place, but that wasn't there then, on the day we're talking about, that is. I took it the gent had just taken the house.'

'I see. You were kind enough, I think, to call me "a man of the world" just now,' said Holmes with a smile. 'I think I may venture to suppose that you are the same, sir, and I would ask you this. How did you read matters between your fare and this lady?'

Mr Maunby considered a long moment. 'Well, sir,' he said judiciously, 'I took it they was man and wife, and she'd run away. He comes after her, asks her to think again, shows her the house he's just taken for the two of them.'

Holmes nodded. 'You are extremely astute,' he said. 'In the circumstances, you will appreciate why I have been called in, and you will further appreciate that your discretion would be much appreciated.' He passed some coins to Mr Maunby, and also to Mr White, who stood listening pretty much open-mouthed. 'Come along, Watson. Good day, gentlemen, and thank you for your help,' and Holmes led the way back to Northumberland Avenue.

'Do you think that fellow had it right, then?' I asked.

'It may well be so,' Holmes answered carelessly. 'It may indeed be that Mr Godfrey Norton has pursued his runaway wife here.' He looked around, and added, 'In any event, if they think at the cab yard that it is merely a case of a runaway wife, they may be less inclined to speculate further in public.'

'I see. In any event, it is certain that the man was not unknown to Mrs Norton, for she showed no fear or surprise at his approach; and she seems to have allowed herself to be persuaded to miss her appointment with you readily enough. Still it is odd, Holmes. I take it we are going to Little William Mews?'

'We are – cab!' Holmes waved at a passing cab, and we climbed aboard. 'Mayfair, driver, Little William Mews, if you please.'

Holmes sat in silence as we rattled along, and indeed I was disinclined to speculate as to what might be behind the very odd circumstances that were coming to light. Could it be nothing more serious than a matrimonial tiff that had brought the erstwhile Miss Adler to consult Holmes? It seemed trivial enough, in all conscience, particularly in view of the oddly worded note she had sent. But then I knew that all sorts of folk consulted my old friend upon all sorts of matters, the trivial as well as the nationally important, the farcical as well as the tragic, and sometimes the language in which their appeals were couched was strange, even melodramatic, in the extreme!

We arrived in Mayfair, and Holmes told the driver not to wait. 'We can get another cab easily enough here,' he told me. 'And it may be that this business will take some considerable time to unravel.'

Number eighteen, Little William Mews, was a typical mews establishment, if perhaps a touch more run-down than its near neighbours. At street level there was a large wooden double door to the stabling, the paint on this door being somewhat the worse for wear; next to this was an ordinary house door, leading to the upper floors where the coachman and his family would normally live. There were no curtains at the windows, though, and the whole place bore every sign of being unoccupied, and in fact of having stood empty for some time.

'Nobody at home, it seems,' I muttered. 'Although there's no "To Let" sign, just as that chap at the yard told us.'

Holmes waved a hand. 'Easy enough to take the place on a short lease, a month, three months, Just long enough –' and he broke off.

'Long enough for what?'

'Long enough, I was about to say, for them to carry out whatever nefarious schemes they had in mind. It does look as if the birds have flown, though, Doctor, as you observe. Still, it may be worth our while just to take a look inside.' So saying, he approached the door that led to the cottage side of the house, and discreetly tried the lock. 'H'mm.' He glanced to one side, and smiled.

I followed his gaze, and saw an iron ladder, evidently intended as a fire escape, bolted to the wall. Looking up, I saw that a first-floor window stood conveniently by the side of this ladder – or, I should say rather, the ladder had been affixed conveniently by the window. The effect was the same, however, and it was only too clear to me just what Holmes had in mind. I began, 'Holmes, you cannot –' but I was too late, he was already shinning up the ladder. I saw him take some implement from his pocket, fumble with the window catch, then throw the window up and climb inside. This was done, I may say, in almost less time than it takes me to write about it.

I glanced round, a touch nervously. It was around the hour of noon, and the various stables and so on round about were quiet, their inhabitants obviously out on the day's work, or inside eating their midday meals. Still, there were one or two loungers in the street, and I hoped fervently that none of them had taken too keen an interest in what Holmes and I were up to.

My musings were interrupted by a sudden shout from the open window. 'Watson! Watson, come quickly, man!'

I did not hesitate, but clambered up the iron ladder, somewhat encumbered by my medical bag – for you will recall that I had been on my way home from my morning rounds when I had become so suddenly and curiously enmeshed in this strange affair. I reached the window, and climbed in. The room was empty of furniture, and bore an air of neglect. Holmes stood there, dishevelled, his face flushed with excitement.

'What is it, Holmes?'

For answer, he grabbed my arm and fairly hauled me into the next room. That too was dusty, empty of furniture save for a single ordinary kitchen chair that stood in the centre of the room. Seated on this chair was Mrs Irene Norton, looking as if she were about to swoon.

As you will readily believe, a good many questions occurred to me; but the important thing at that moment was to attend to Mrs Norton. It is no insult to my own dear wife to say that the former Miss Adler was a beautiful creature, lovely of face and figure, and with long, lustrous hair that would be the envy of many a Society beauty. Now, though, her face was pale, save for a livid bruise on one side, and there were great dusky patches under her eyes. On the floor by the chair in which she sat there were a couple of lengths of rope. 'They had bound and gagged her,' said Holmes, seeing me glance at these ropes.

'The villains!' I hastily examined Mrs Norton. She was weak, and there were some slight abrasions on her wrists, and that bruise on her face, but I could see no real damage.

I held some smelling-salts under her nose, but she waved me away. 'If I might have a little water?' she asked, faintly. 'I have neither eaten nor drunk these two days.'

'Of course! Holmes, could you –' but he was already gone, returning a moment later with water in a large, cracked, and slightly grubby cup.

'Best I could –'

'Oh, Mr Holmes, no champagne ever tasted better!' Mrs

Norton told him. 'Or sherry either! I shall need no aperitif to make me want my supper tonight!'

'Drink slowly,' I told her.

Holmes asked, 'Watson?'

'Oh, Mrs Norton is a little fatigued, a little dehydrated, and, as she has delicately hinted, ravenously hungry! But nothing more serious than that, I fancy.'

'It is as well,' said Holmes, a grimness in his tone and upon his features that boded ill for whoever was responsible for abducting Mrs Norton and leaving her in such a state. 'Can you walk, madam? Or –'

'I can walk, Mr Holmes. Perhaps a drop more water?'

Holmes brought more from the kitchen downstairs, and I added the merest splash of brandy, for it was clear that Mrs Norton, despite her bantering tone, was very weak.

We assisted her down the rickety stairs, and Holmes fiddled with the lock of the cottage door, muttering, 'I shall make good any damage later,' as he forced it open.

I went out first, and was about to offer Mrs Norton my arm when I became aware that we had attracted a quite sizeable crowd. Evidently those loungers whom I had noticed earlier had given the alarm, and the local inhabitants had turned out in force to confront what they must have thought was a gang of burglars. A commendable and public-spirited action, to be sure, but it looked a trifle awkward for Holmes and me. A couple of rough-looking men headed the group, one of whom swung in his hand a large iron spike. I remember thinking – rather foolishly perhaps – that it must be some instrument for removing stones from horses' hooves; certainly it could do some nasty damage to a man's head. I was about to speak, when from the back of the crowd a voice which I recognized called out, 'Here, enough of that! I'll take charge here!'

'Lestrade! Is that you?' I asked.

The wiry figure of our old friend Inspector Lestrade of Scotland Yard elbowed its way through the crowd. 'What's more to the point, is that you, Doctor Watson? Lord, it is! What the – that is, what on earth are you doing here? And Mr Holmes, too, and with a lady?'

'Nothing that would concern you, Lestrade,' said Holmes crisply. 'There may be some trifling damage to the lock of this door, for which I shall stand good. That aside, it is merely a case of a dispute between husband and wife.'

'Oh, a "domestic" case, is it?' said Lestrade, somewhat disappointed. 'If that's so, I'll clear off, for whoever is in the right in such matters, we – the police – are invariably in the wrong! I've known a couple fight like cat and dog, and then team up to bean the constable who tried to interfere.' This was said, I might add, in such a tone as to suggest that Lestrade himself had been 'beaned' more than once at some early stage in his career. 'I'll get a locksmith, Mr Holmes, and have him send you the bill.'

'Please do, Lestrade. If we might have a cab?'

And before too long, we were all three in a cab and headed for Baker Street. Mrs Norton tried more than once to say something, but neither Holmes nor I would allow her to agitate herself. Arrived at 221B, I summoned an astonished Mrs Hudson, and ordered beef tea at once, and a little steamed fish later, such being the only supper I would countenance for Mrs Norton for the moment.

We escorted the lady to Holmes's rooms, and placed her in the best armchair. 'Mrs Hudson will be here with your beef tea before too long,' I said. 'And when you are stronger, and have had something to eat –' and I broke off, looking at Holmes. 'It would hardly be seemly, Holmes, for Mrs Norton

27

to remain here. And an hotel, even the Northumberland, is a touch impersonal, given the shock Mrs Norton has had.'

He nodded. 'I believe you have a spare room, Doctor? If your wife were agreeable –'

'Oh, have no fears on that score, Holmes,' I told him. I noticed that Mrs Norton was making some effort to interrupt me. 'Pray do not exert yourself, dear lady,' I said. 'Whatever it may be, it can wait a little while.'

'Oh, but it cannot! It really cannot! Mr Holmes, Doctor Watson, you must go at once!'

'Go?' asked Holmes. 'Go where?'

'Why, to Bohemia, of course! Mr Holmes, you must save the king!'

TWO

As a general rule, Mr Sherlock Holmes is not easily shocked, nor does he lack for words in most situations. Now, however, he floundered almost as badly as I was floundering myself. 'To Bohemia?' said he. 'Why, I hardly – Watson?' And he shot me a glance full of meaning.

'Yes, you are right, Holmes. The strain of the past few days –'

Mrs Norton broke in, 'No, no, Doctor! I understand that you think it is some foolishness engendered by my ordeal, there is nothing else you could think, but I assure you that nothing could be further from the truth.' She stopped, and put a hand to her brow.

'You are fatigued, madam,' I began, but any further remarks were cut short by the entrance of Mrs Hudson, bearing a tray with that beef tea which I had ordered, along with some of her tiny cheese scones.

'I thought, Doctor, that the lady might manage a bite to eat,' said Mrs Hudson.

'Not too much, mind,' I cautioned. As Mrs Hudson fussed round Mrs Norton, I drew Holmes to one side. 'It seems clear, Holmes, that the events of the past two days have indeed unsettled the poor lady, revived memories of the king –'

A little laugh interrupted me. 'At any rate, Doctor Watson,

the strain has not affected my hearing, which always was acute!' said Mrs Norton. 'No, Mrs Hudson, that will be excellent! I can manage for myself, now. Thank you so much.' As Mrs Hudson shot an angry glance at Holmes and myself, and left the room, Mrs Norton went on, 'I can understand how it must seem, but I assure you that I am not wandering in my mind. The king is indeed in grave danger, and I suspect that you are the only men who can save him.'

'If that is so,' said Holmes, sinking into a chair opposite Mrs Norton, 'then we shall need to know something of what brought you here to London in the first instance, and also something more specific as to what happened two days past.'

Mrs Norton nodded. 'If I might speak as I eat, for I am very hungry?' And, as she ate the tasty morsels Mrs Hudson had provided, and sipped the beef tea, Mrs Norton went on, 'I need hardly dwell at length on the old case, as you would call it, but I must tell you something of how matters stood between myself and the King of Bohemia. I was, as you know, born in America, the youngest child of an immigrant family. We were "poor but honest", as the newspapers put it, and my parents had something of a struggle in their early days in the new country. And by the time I was born, although their circumstances had improved somewhat, they were by no means rich. From being a little girl I enjoyed singing, and as I grew up I found that I had a talent in that direction. I might have stayed in America, but instead I chose to come to Europe, and I found work at La Scala, and later at Warsaw.'

'That much we know.'

Mrs Norton smiled. 'I quickly realized that although I

was – am – what might charitably be called "competent" or "adequate", I should never be a singer in the first rank.'

Holmes made as if to speak, then waved a hand for her to continue.

'Mr Holmes?'

'Forgive me. I had understood you were highly thought of at Warsaw?'

Mrs Norton smiled. 'I had some success, it is true. But I had no illusions – other, younger, better, singers were waiting in the wings. Besides, I thought – well! Being of a practical turn of mind, I decided that there were but two choices open to me. I might return to America, to try whether the competition there was as stiff as in Europe; or I might marry for money. I chose the latter course. Quite coldly, quite deliberately. I began to look around for the right man, and I found him, in the shape of the – then – Crown Prince of Bohemia. We met, talked, dined. And – and I found that my grand design had come to nought. For I fell in love with him! And, truth to tell, I cannot believe that any woman alive would not have fallen in love with him.'

(At this point, I mentally pictured the king as I had known him, six foot odd of self-opinionated sulks, though handsome enough in a coarse sort of fashion; and I reflected sadly that this last remark was probably quite true. I fear that something of Holmes's cynicism has rubbed off over the years, as indeed it was bound to do.) Mrs Norton was saying, 'He was generous – in truth, as I began to tell you a moment ago, I fancy that my success was due indirectly to him, for the authorities at Warsaw were anxious to please him, and my rapid promotion could not, by the most charitable, be ascribed to my innate talent. Be that as it may, he promised me marriage, of course. And I am sure that the promise was seriously intended, that he had simply not thought the matter out properly. In his defence, and indeed in my own, I must add that we were very young.'

'You are hardly old now, madam,' I told her.

She smiled. 'Thank you, Doctor.' The smile vanished. 'Then the world intruded upon us. The king, as he became, was expected to marry for reasons of state, for political expediency, for the good of his country and his people. There was, it is true, the possibility of – of some informal arrangement between us, but you will appreciate that I declined that offer.'

'I should think so, too!' I said.

Holmes said, 'And it was then that you decided to send a compromising photograph to the king's bride-to-be?'

Mrs Norton shook her head quickly. 'Pray hear me out, Mr Holmes, before you judge me. I could, I think, accept that the king must marry as his ministers directed, and as his country's good demanded. And although I declined it, I was not offended by the suggestion of a continued, illicit liaison after the marriage – truth to tell, the king made the suggestion not in any base spirit, but rather because he was reluctant, just as I was myself, to abandon the happiness we had known. No, I would have burned his letters, and the photograph, had I not met a – a man, I suppose I should say, but "devil" would be nearer the mark!'

'What, Godfrey Norton?' asked Holmes at once.

Mrs Norton laughed. 'Godfrey? No, Mr Holmes, if you knew him, you would know why I laugh. Why, Godfrey is the sweetest, the gentlest, the best of men. No, the man I met was of another sort altogether. His name is Karl-Heinz Siebald, known as Karl, but he sometimes styles himself Karl-Heinz von Ormstein. He is the king's elder brother.'

Holmes and I stared at her. 'But –'

Mrs Norton raised a hand. 'The king's roving eye was evidently inherited,' she told us drily.

'Ah!' said Holmes, sinking back in his chair.

'Yes,' said Mrs Norton with a nod. 'The old king, that is Wilhelm's father, whilst still a young man, became enamoured of a Fräulein Siebald, daughter of a wealthy and respectable commoner. There was a child, but there could be no marriage. Then the king was informed that a suitable bride had been found. He married the lady, and in due course of time Wilhelm was born. The old king did what he could for Karl. His name he could not give, nor rank; but he made him a most generous allowance, on condition that Karl should leave Bohemia when he reached fifteen years of age, and never return again to the land of his birth. And in a secret ceremony the old king bestowed on Karl the highest of Bohemia's honours, the Grand Cordon of the Order of Saint Wenceslas. Karl moved to Paris, to live an aimless life, a life of pleasure. Or so it appeared, though I now suspect that it was a careful act, intended to fool the world.'

'H'mm,' said Holmes. 'One might perhaps have expressed the wish that those circumstances had not arisen; but given that they did arise, I think the old king's actions would be deemed generous by most men.'

'Not by Karl,' said Mrs Norton.

'Ahah! So, this Karl persuaded you to spoil the new king's chances of marriage?'

Mrs Norton nodded. 'I was a fool ever to listen to him. I know that now. But he was very plausible.'

'It is ever the way with rogues,' said Holmes, somewhat sententiously.

'It was in Paris that I met him first. After the break with the king I was spending a little time in the city, trying to think matters over, and Karl made himself known to me. Of course I had no idea of his parentage, not at first. He entertained me lavishly, but behaved like a perfect gentleman, quite unlike the man he had the reputation of being. And then one day he mentioned his past. Naturally I was taken aback. I could sympathize with him, and said as much. Before I knew it, I had told him something of my own unhappy experiences. And then Karl said something to the effect that we had both been wronged by the royal house of von Ormstein. I listened to him – would that I had not, that I had never allowed him to set foot in the house! But I did.' Mrs Norton flushed, and shrugged her shoulders. 'In truth, I needed but little persuasion. What woman, wronged as I had been wronged, would need overmuch convincing that the man who had wronged her should suffer as well?

'I had thought it the merest chance, my meeting Karl as I did, and the fact that we had so much, as it seemed, in common. Now I believe that he had arranged it all, that his spies had somehow discovered about the king and my unhappy self, and that Karl had decided to use me to hurt his half-brother, and sought me out accordingly. Well, the rest you know, I fancy. I came to London, absolutely determined to send the letters and photograph to the old King of Scandinavia, and thereby wreck the King of Bohemia's marriage.

'Then I met Godfrey, and fell in love with him. I had all but decided to destroy the king's letters and the photograph, when the king foolishly attempted to take them from me by force! His creatures waylaid me, laid their grimy hands upon me, bullied me, searched me. All my old anger flared up at once, and I made my mind up; I should send the photograph after all! Then you came on the scene, Mr Holmes, and when I talked the matter over one last time with Godfrey, he convinced me that it would be best to leave the country, forget all about the king, and let events in Bohemia turn out as they might. I agreed. After all, I had my happiness; why should I begrudge the king his, though he had wronged me most grievously?'

'And this Karl?'

'Oh, I never saw him again, or not until two days ago.'

'And then?'

'Bear with me, Mr Holmes. I had put the matter out of my mind as much as I reasonably could, and Godfrey and I had more or less settled down on the Continent. His family, I may say, are well-to-do, and Godfrey has a substantial private income, so we have no worries on that score. However, a few weeks ago, there was a clumsy burglary, or attempt at burglary, at our house. I knew at once that it was the papers that were the object of the attempt. And I knew also that the king, and you, Mr Holmes, would never try anything of the kind.'

'You might rely on me,' Holmes interrupted, 'but how could you be sure that it was not the king?'

'He wrote me a note, when I was settled on the Continent. A formal little note, no seal, signed only with the initial "W", so that no-one might know who had sent it. But I knew. He told me that he was sorry things had come to the pass that they had come to, and that he trusted me implicitly. He swore there was nothing to fear from him. I believed him, Mr Holmes. And so I knew, you see, that Karl was behind the bungled robbery.'

'Forgive me,' I put in, 'but I am confused. If Karl is – from the wrong side of the blanket, as they say – then he cannot gain from the king's disgrace. Indeed, this Karl could not inherit the throne, even if the king were to die. Or have I missed something?'

'Hate and revenge are powerful motives enough, Doctor,' said Holmes.

'True,' added Mrs Norton, 'but there is yet a third. Karl has an ally. Gottfried Baldur von Ormstein, Duke of Essen-Württemburg, the king's cousin, and – in the absence of a son, a crown prince – the heir to the throne.'

'I see,' said Holmes. 'They hope somehow to get rid of the king, set this Gottfried on the throne, and divide the contents of the treasury – I perhaps put the matter crudely, but I fancy that is what it amounts to – between them?'

Mrs Norton nodded.

I said, 'Again, I am puzzled. The king is crowned, and married. Even though there is, as yet, no son and heir, surely the only way these conspirators could put their own man on the throne is by killing the king? Why, then, do they need letters, a compromising photograph, and the like?'

Holmes nodded at this. 'Well put, Doctor.'

Mrs Norton said, 'They do not propose to kill the king, but to bring about his disgrace, and thus his abdication. You must understand that the king's reputation to some extent preceded him in the matter of his marriage. There was to be a treaty, greatly to Bohemia's commercial advantage, with the family of his bride. But the King of Scandinavia, mindful of the tales he had heard of Wilhelm – the King of Bohemia, that is – would not sign the treaty until two years after the wedding. Ostensibly this was to give everyone "time to think it over, to finalize the details", as the King of

Scandinavia put it; in reality, it was to test the fidelity and probity of the King of Bohemia.'

'Ah!' said I. 'So if the King of Bohemia behaves himself for two years – less, now – then the treaty will be signed. If not, then the King of Scandinavia, the other party to the treaty, will simply refuse to sign. That it?'

'You sum it up admirably, Doctor,' said Mrs Norton. 'You may know that the politics of Bohemia, like those of many another middle European state, are very unsettled at the moment. There are many factions, some urging closer links with Austria-Hungary, some urging a treaty with France, even England. And there is a strong military faction which would like to see Bohemia expanding in Europe by force of arms, perhaps in an alliance with Prussia. I may add in passing that this military faction, though aggressive in its outlook, is fanatically loyal to the king, and would take a dim view of anyone who aimed to gain the throne by assassination. And besides that, the generals and colonels favour as an heir – in the absence of a crown prince only, of course – a young soldier, one Maurice von Ormstein, a distant relative of the king, loyal like the rest of the army, but still with some claim to the throne. If Wilhelm died by violence or in suspicious circumstances, then the army would support Maurice's claim; but if Wilhelm abdicated and named Gottfried his successor, the army, loyal to Wilhelm as it is, would transfer that loyalty to Gottfried. For that reason, Gottfried and Karl balk at the notion of killing Wilhelm, and want him to abdicate.

'Very well, to resume my story; two years ago, faced with these various disputing factions, the prime minister, Adolphus von Mitternacht, devised a brilliant scheme – a marriage, and a treaty with Scandinavia, which would fill Bohemia's coffers whilst not antagonizing any of the conflicting factions. But the treaty is dependent upon the marriage. Had there been a crown prince, of course, then matters might be different. As it is, should there be any scandal, should Karl send the photograph to the King of Scandinavia so that he refuses to sign the treaty, there will undoubtedly be open rebellion. The king will be obliged to abdicate in favour of Gottfried, or see Bohemia plunged into civil war.'

'The king might abdicate and name this Maurice, though?' said Holmes.

Mrs Norton shook her head. 'Not when Gottfried's claim is the stronger! There would be bloodshed, I assure you. Even if the army prevailed and set Maurice upon the throne, Bohemia would be ruined, half her people dead.'

'That explains a good deal,' I told her. 'The King of Bohemia, you know, forbade any publication of my accounts for a period of two years. I wondered why he was so very particular about that length of time, but this makes all clear.'

Holmes interrupted, 'Be that as it may, you had not finished your tale, madam?'

'No, but there remains only a little more. I knew, as I say, that Karl was trying to gain possession of the papers. I could not consult His Majesty; so I therefore determined to come here and consult you, Mr Holmes.'

'Which you failed to do?'

'Which I failed to do.'

'Thanks to Karl I take it. Or to one of his agents, perhaps?'

'No, it was Karl himself. He was waiting outside my hotel, and he spoke to me. I told him that I was unhappy with his actions, and he replied that he understood my concerns, but he could explain them away easily enough, if

I would accompany him to his lodgings. I hesitated, for I had my suspicions even then, but he was as persuasive as ever. "What could I lose?" was the burden of his song; if he failed to explain matters, I could still take whatever action I might see fit. Foolishly I agreed. We went to that dreadful place, and I must have looked askance at the room. Karl explained that he had just taken the place, and not had time to furnish it. He offered me his flask, and I took a sip – no more, I swear it! At once, I felt myself swooning. The brandy was drugged, of course. Then I knew no more until I woke up, and found myself bound and gagged, much as you discovered me, Karl was there, grinning at me. The papers were all he wanted, he said, if I told him where they were, then I might go free. I was half-conscious, still under the effects of the drug, and so believed him. More, when I managed to pull my scattered wits together slightly, I actually thought that when once I were free, I could come to you, Mr Holmes, and there would be time enough to do something, to take action to recover the papers! I told him where to find the papers, then, and he – he replaced the gag and he left me there!' She buried her head in her hands.

'The fellow is a pretty hardened villain,' I said hotly. 'But why did he not kill you out of hand, make sure you could not tell anyone what had happened?'

'He is what you would call squeamish,' said Mrs Norton. 'He dared not trust an agent, but he would keep his own hands clean – if you can call them clean.'

'Still, he could not know that we would find you,' said Holmes. 'This Karl is, as Watson says, not a very pleasant fellow.'

'All the more reason why you should not delay!' said Mrs Norton rather sharply.

Holmes shook his head quickly. 'I appreciate your concern for the king's future,' he said. 'But you forget that we have in effect lost two whole days. The photograph might well be on its way to the King of Scandinavia now. It might already be on His Majesty's desk, staring at him whilst he composes a stern formal note to his son-in-law!'

It was Mrs Norton's turn to shake her head. 'That is not how it will be handled, as I have told you.'

'Very well,' said Holmes. 'But then a copy of the photograph might have been sent to the King of Bohemia. The instrument of abdication might be drawn up already.'

Mrs Norton shook her head again. 'Even if the king has already been threatened, if the very instrument of abdication has indeed been drawn up ready to be signed, by prompt action you might still save the situation. In any event, I think there may yet be time enough. I suspect that Gottfried and Karl will not have acted yet, and for this reason. The first anniversary of the king's marriage is in the middle of April. The King of Scandinavia will attend the celebrations, to wish the couple success publicly. And in private, to reassure himself that his son-in-law is behaving himself! That is when Karl and Gottfried will want Wilhelm to abdicate. In public, and whilst the King of Scandinavia is in Bohemia. That way, there will be an independent witness to say that Wilhelm left the throne voluntarily. And I suspect that Gottfried will press the King of Scandinavia to sign the treaty there and then. That will have the effect of confirming Gottfried's position.'

'And the two years' delay?' I asked.

'Oh, Gottfried is very different from Wilhelm!' said Mrs Norton. 'Gottfried's life is above reproach; the King of Scandinavia would not hesitate to sign a treaty with him, I assure you.'

'Given that you have read it right,' said Holmes, 'what would you have me do?'

'Go to Bohemia, as I said, and take action to save the king! You have some five or six weeks. God grant that it may be sufficient time, even for you, Mr Holmes.'

Holmes looked doubtful. 'This precious pair, the Karl who abducted you and left you to live or die as chance should dictate, and this other, Gottfried, they will have servants, allies, I take it?'

'Of course.'

'And this Gottfried doubtless has a house, lands, an estate?'

'A veritable castle, Mr Holmes. But why do you ask?'

'They know the country, the language –'

'Oh, German is widely spoken, and universally understood!'

'But their forces are considerably stronger than mine,' Holmes pointed out. 'It is not that I am afraid, madam, but rather that it is as well to form a realistic view of one's chances.'

'You forget, Mr Holmes, that you would have one staunch ally,' said Mrs Norton.

'You? Hardly, madam! I yield to no man in my admiration for the modern woman, but this is man's work.'

'Clearly!' said I, with what scorn I could muster. 'Only a complete fool would fail to realize that Mrs Norton meant me!'

'You, Watson? But your wife, your practice –'

'Leave all that to me, Holmes. Now, where is your Bradshaw? We can probably get a boat train tonight, and –'

Mrs Norton coughed, delicately but with meaning. 'I

was referring neither to myself, nor to Doctor Watson,' she told us severely.

'Who, then?' asked Holmes.

'Why, to Wilhelm! The king, that is to say. He will, naturally, be anxious to do what he might to help.'

'Ah, the king, to be sure,' said Holmes. 'You are right, of course, madam. And I think that lets you out, Watson. A fact for which Mrs Watson will be grateful, no doubt.'

'Oh, so that's what you think, is it, Holmes? Well, you can think again! I shall not dream of letting you wander about the Continent on your own.'

'But your practice?'

'Oh, things are quieter now than they have been. Anstruther or Jackson would handle my work. They have both done so often enough in the past. If they are busy, they can divide it between them, come to that.'

'And your wife?'

'Ah.' I thought a moment. 'Mary will understand perfectly, I feel sure. That is, once I have explained matters to her.'

'My own needs are few,' said Holmes, standing up and consulting a railway timetable. 'Yes, we have a few hours yet. Plenty of time to take Mrs Norton here to your house, Watson.'

'Oh, but surely there is no need?' said Mrs Norton. 'Now that you are going, Mr Holmes, there can be no objection to my remaining here? And, indeed, I might just as well return to my hotel, or go back home to Godfrey! He will be missing me, I know. I want to be no trouble to anyone, least of all to dear Mrs Watson!'

'No trouble at all,' I said.

And Holmes shook his head. 'This Karl may return, to

see what has become of you. Or he might send one of his agents. Should he learn that you are not dead, that you have escaped, this is the first place he will look. And your hotel, and your home, will be next on the list. I will be much happier if I know that you are safe with Mrs Watson.'

'Well, if you positively insist, Mr Holmes.'

'If you will allow me a moment to pack my bag?' said Holmes. 'Then we shall arrange a small subterfuge. It will, I fear, mean that you must forgo Mrs Hudson's excellent steamed fish, madam, but I am sure that Mrs Watson's cook will provide something equally digestible and nutritious.'

'It was to have been Lancashire hot-pot tonight!' I muttered, not without a tinge of regret.

'Oh, if you're hungry you can buy a sandwich at Victoria, or somewhere,' said Holmes, in his most offensive tone. 'There remains but one question, Mrs Norton. In all our dealings with the King of Bohemia, and with yourself, we have often mentioned this photograph, or heard it mentioned, but we have not the slightest notion of what it depicts, other than that the king and yourself are both in the photograph.'

'The papers which Karl has stolen are contained in a morocco leather document case, blue in colour and about this size,' said Mrs Norton, indicating with her hands a rectangle of some ten inches by eight. 'They consist of the king's letters to me, twenty-three of them, if we are to be precise –'

'By all means let us be precise,' said Holmes.

'Very well. Twenty-three letters, then, in the king's hand, sealed with red wax, his crest embossed in the seals. They, of course, are of lesser importance, for they might be laughed off as forgeries. The king's writing, though distinctive, perhaps even florid, is not difficult of imitation; the paper, with the royal watermark, might have been stolen; and as for the crest, the double-headed eagle of the von Ormsteins, its duplicate might be seen in a dozen second-hand jewellery shops in Clerkenwell. The important thing is the photograph. As for its subject –' and here Mrs Norton fumbled in the bosom of her dress, and produced an ordinary cabinet-sized photographic print, which she handed to Holmes.

He studied it intently, and I leaned over his shoulder to look. The photograph had every appearance of having been taken by an enthusiastic amateur. It showed a young couple seated in a boat, a steam launch by the look of it, on what was pretty clearly the Rhine, for the background showed the sort of high wooded cliffs that you see there, and there was even a ruined schloss in the far distance. The king was dressed in flannel trousers and a striped blazer, and had a straw hat on his head; Miss Adler, as she had then been, wore a summer dress in the style popular some five years previously, and was hatless, her long hair tumbling about her shoulders. She gazed up at the king, who himself had turned his head to glance down at her. As I gazed at the king's face, all the sardonic thoughts that had passed through my mind earlier were driven out, for it was obvious that he was head over heels in love with Miss Adler. It was equally obvious that she adored him. All in all, they might have been any young, loving couple who had just got married or engaged. More to the point, nobody who saw that photograph would ever believe that the king could possibly love another woman as he had loved Miss Adler! I saw at once that therein lay the great danger it represented to the king's happiness.

'Who took the photograph?' I asked.

'Oh, Bertie. Bertram von Gratz, I mean. A great friend of the king's, who was on holiday with us then.'

Holmes said, 'Irrespective of the identity of the photographer, how do you come to retain this, madam?'

'Yes!' I added. 'And if you have the photograph, then what the – that is, what has Karl got?'

'Karl has the original plate,' said Mrs Norton quietly. 'What the photographers call the "negative", I believe. You see, a clever mechanic might even have faked the photograph, and that is what the king would claim were it only the prints that were in existence. His Majesty could, and would, call his own experts to swear that this print was bogus, and all its fellows too. But the original plate will show clearly that it is genuine. With that, Karl may make a hundred copies, if he will.'

'Odd that he didn't spot this print, though?' I mused.

'Oh, but he did,' said Mrs Norton. 'Or, rather, he gave it to me.'

'Oh?' Holmes and I spoke together.

'Yes. He returned yesterday, bringing the picture with him. I think it was to taunt me, to show me that he actually had the papers. He tucked the picture in my dress, saying that if – when – I were discovered, the photograph would merely add to the king's disgrace. Did I not say as much just now?'

'No, madam, you did not,' said Holmes.

'Oh, but I was so faint! I must have forgotten.'

I was unconvinced by this, and half expected Holmes to make some further remark, but all he said was, 'Very understandable, given the circumstances. And you want me to follow Karl, recover the plate, and hand it to the king before any harm is done?'

'To me, Mr Holmes,' said Mrs Norton quickly.

'But would it not be safer in the king's hands?'

Mrs Norton smiled wanly. 'You see how much trouble the wretched thing has caused already, Mr Holmes! My fear has always been that the king, possibly influenced by one of his ministers, would attempt to do me some harm. The photograph is my only security, and even then it has not been wholly reliable. I shall not feel safe until I have it back, and can make some proper arrangements for its safe-keeping.'

'I understand perfectly,' said Holmes. He glanced at me, and went on, 'Now I must get my things together. Watson, might I trouble you to borrow a hat and scarf of Mrs Hudson's?'

In a very short while we were ready. Holmes ignored Mrs Hudson's protests that the steamed fish was ready and would spoil, and sauntered out into the street, while I stood watching from a side window. When Holmes signalled that all was well, I took Mrs Norton, suitably disguised in an old hat and shawl, out to the cab which Holmes had summoned.

'I saw no-one,' said Holmes as we rattled along towards Paddington, and my own little house. 'But then there is no reason why Karl, or anyone else, should suspect that Mrs Norton is at liberty.'

Arrived at my small establishment, I quickly explained the situation to my wife. She is perhaps the kindest of women – I can undertake that she is certainly the most understanding! 'Of course Mrs Norton must stay here,' said Mary. She added with a brave little smile, 'And of course you must go with Mr Sherlock Holmes to save the poor king.'

I thought it best to refrain from pointing out that the king had, when all was said and done, only himself to blame for his predicament, and murmured something appropriately platitudinous.

Holmes is not normally particularly sensitive to the feelings of others, but he seemed to perceive that Mary was not entirely happy at the thought of my leaving her in this way. With a reassuring glance, he told her, 'I promise you, Mrs Watson, that I shall take the greatest care of the good doctor. I am sure you must be anxious, and indeed it is a great deal that I ask of Watson – and of you – but perhaps I might have a private word, and try to allay any misgivings?'

'It is quite unnecessary, Mr Holmes,' said Mary, but he took her arm gently and steered her into a quiet corner. I, meanwhile, took the opportunity to have a word with Mrs Norton, suggesting rest and a light diet for a day or so, and prescribing a mild restorative and also a sleeping draught, as I felt that the horrors of the past couple of days might return when darkness fell.

I looked up to see Holmes escort Mary back to the centre of the room. 'So you see, you may rely upon me,' he said, with a bow.

'And you upon me,' said Mary, with a laugh. 'To look after Mrs Norton, I mean.'

'Well, Watson?'

'I am all but ready,' I told him. 'I shall just throw a few things into a bag, and I'm your man. Call a cab, if you wish, for I shan't be long.'

Holmes glanced at Mary, who was fussing round Mrs Norton, and followed me out of the room. I dashed upstairs, fully expecting that Holmes would do as I asked him, and go out into the street to call a cab, and then return to the ladies. I was thus somewhat astonished when, as I was putting the finishing touches to my hasty packing, I looked up to see him enter the bedroom and put a finger to his lips.

'Holmes?'

'What do you think to Mrs Norton, Watson?'

I stared at him. 'Attractive, of course –'

'I meant, what do you think to her story?'

'Oh, the story! Well –' I hesitated. 'What do you think, Holmes?'

'I think it very odd that someone tied up in a chair, bound and gagged and left to starve to death, should entirely forget that their tormentor had returned the next day in order to torment them further!'

'Oh, that might be the strain, the shock –'

Holmes waved a hand impatiently. 'The crux, the very heart, of this whole matter is the photograph, Watson. Would Mrs Norton fail to recollect that she had the photograph, or a copy of it, about her person? Why, I believe that if we had not mentioned the photograph, she would never have shown it to us! How believable is that?'

I shrugged. 'I can only repeat, Holmes, that the shock may have had something to do with it.'

'You may be right,' said he lightly. 'It may, as you say, be the effects of her ordeal. But then tell me this – why should this mysterious "Karl" reveal the address to the driver of the cab?'

'He could hardly expect to be taken there without giving the address!' I pointed out with a smile.

Holmes regarded me severely.

'Sorry, Holmes. I take your meaning, that the kidnapper could, and should, have given a more vague address, have walked with Mrs Norton from the next street or something of the sort. But then this Karl may not have realized that Mrs Norton was in London to consult you? He may have thought that he had no reason to conceal the real address?'

Holmes nodded. 'I concede the point, though a clever man, as I take this Karl to be, would surely have made the logical deduction? Why else would Mrs Norton visit London, but to see me? I hasten to add that I ask the question not for any vainglorious reason, but because the Nortons have cut themselves off so thoroughly from England. If it were, let us say, a family visit, why should Godfrey Norton not be here along with his wife? It is his immediate family, not hers, when all is said and done.'

'H'mm. One thing I can say, Holmes, without fear of contradiction, and that is that Mrs Norton was indeed suffering from fatigue, and was in some very real distress. I have worked for too long in the poorer quarters of the city not to know that when I see it. Of course, I cannot say just what the cause of that distress may have been, but it was real enough, I'll swear to that.'

'I would not venture to contradict you, Watson.' He stared into space for a long moment, then shook his head. 'It may be genuine, the tale may be true. The anomalies I think I see may all be accident, coincidence, as you suggest.'

I regarded him closely. 'But you do not believe that? You think she is lying to us?'

'In my own mind, I am certain of it.'

'But then what do you think is behind it? Did Mrs Norton and this Karl – if "Karl" indeed it was – engineer the whole business? Did they intend us to "rescue" Mrs Norton, then? And if so, why?'

Holmes shook his head. 'There you have me, Watson.

The obvious reason behind such an elaborate charade would be to gain our sympathy, to convince us that Mrs Norton is telling the truth, to make us believe implicitly in whatever she might choose to tell us.'

'Again, I ask "why?" Holmes.'

He shook his head a second time. 'It is, I fear, beyond me for the moment. We have insufficient data. In any event, you may be perfectly correct, it may have been a genuine error on Mrs Norton's part, due entirely to the ordeal she has been through. By the way, Doctor,' he added in the inconsequential way he sometimes had, 'I seem to recollect that just before your marriage I saw you perusing the advertisement pages of various journals with a view to taking out a life insurance policy. Did you do so?'

'Why, yes. It seemed sensible, what with getting married, assuming the responsibility for a wife, and what have you. The "Clerical and Medical" people got my modest trade, as seeming the most appropriate, and I have a couple of small policies with them. But why on earth – oh!' and I sat down heavily on the bed.

Holmes nodded. 'There may be some small risk, Doctor. I have some reservations –'

'The only reservations that you need concern yourself about are our tickets for the ferry!' I told him.

He silently shook me by the hand, then leaned over and peered into my shabby suitcase. 'If you omit that pair of socks, Watson, and perhaps a couple of the spare collars, you will make room for your revolver,' said he. 'And a box, no, two boxes, of cartridges.'

THREE

Marriage is a grand thing, no denying that, and I shall defend it as an institution until my last dying breath. But as I sat there in the train with Holmes, polishing my old service revolver – for Holmes had, in his mysterious way, managed to secure a compartment that was unoccupied save for our two selves, and there was no fellow passenger to look askance at my refurbishing of the trusty old weapon – I found myself whistling an old military air quietly, and all the old familiar thrill of the chase came upon me. I smiled to myself at the thought that I had used the word 'old' in my thoughts more times than I would dare to use it on the printed page. But what of that? For this was indeed just like old times, to be sure; nay, better, for at the end of the day, when the excitement and adventure was over and done with, I had a wife and a home to go back to! It had been too long by far since I had been involved in one of Mr Sherlock Holmes's cases, I told myself. Then, too, it was just the sort of case I liked, plenty of excitement, not too much of Holmes's usual sitting about speculating on abstract matters of this and that –

I became aware of Holmes's sardonic eye fixed firmly upon me. 'Well, Holmes?'

'You seem remarkably happy, Watson.'

'And why should I not be? I was just now reflecting that it is like old times, Holmes. Just the sort of adventure that I like, too. I've never been a great one for thinking – and none of your cheap sarcasm, Holmes! I meant only that I prefer something tangible to work at.'

'Indeed, Watson. "A man of action" would cover it, I think.' He smiled. 'And in all sincerity, one could ask for no better man of action than you, Doctor. I am not sorry to have you with me, I confess, for your help may well be invaluable.'

'Good of you to say so.' I hesitated. 'Only one point slightly mars things for me, Holmes. If, as you suspect, Mrs Norton is playing some deep game, then might Mary not be in some danger?'

Holmes shook his head. 'If I thought that for a moment, I should never have allowed Mrs Norton into your house, Watson. No, if I am wrong and Mrs Norton is sincere, there is no danger. If I am right then I fancy that Mrs Norton will lose no time in absconding, for she will have business to occupy her elsewhere. Did you not mark the way in which she protested when I suggested her staying with your wife? She was all for returning to the Continent, and I suspect that is where her gaze will turn. Either way, Mrs Watson will be quite safe.'

I heaved a positive sigh of relief. 'You have quite settled my mind, and I can give my undivided attention to the task before us. Anything I can do, Holmes. You have but to name it.'

He smiled. 'I fear there is little either of us can do just for the moment.' He produced a small fat book with a red cover. 'I acquired this at the station. It is the latest guide to the region, and I shall take the opportunity to study it whilst we are travelling.' And with a nod, he plunged into the little book.

I loaded my revolver, put it away, and gazed out of the window. The flat coastal lands were far behind us now, and the train was going through little German villages set among hills and valleys. It was still only afternoon, perhaps four o'clock, but at that season and in that locality the light was beginning to fade and folk were lighting their lamps. Here and there beyond the neat little houses the last glimmerings of the setting sun lit up the still bare upper branches of great trees, the outer edges of that primeval forest which is such an integral part of the German soul, which sits so deep in the national character. An impressive place, the Schwarzwald, in certain circumstances a grim place, I imagine, and irresistibly I found myself recalling stirring old tales of its legendary inhabitants, the ancient gods and heroes.

'What are you thinking now, Watson?'

'I was just wondering what the restaurants are like in Vienna,' I told him; no use getting poetic where Holmes is concerned.

Holmes smiled and put away his guide book. 'Remarkably good, as I remember. You will have ample opportunity to prove them for yourself tonight, Watson, for there is no connection before tomorrow.'

'Oh good – ah, good gracious, that is a pity, Holmes.'

We stayed in Vienna that night, though I cannot recall just where, nor what we had to eat. I do remember that Holmes picked rather irritably at his food and seemed to be fretting at every wasted moment. And I recall that the German beer was deceptively light, and that the full effect was somewhat postponed, as it were. A fact that was brought home to me at some unearthly hour next morning, when Holmes all but dragged me from my bed, mumbling some nonsense about wanting to catch an early train.

After a grossly inadequate breakfast of milky coffee and a couple of crescent-shaped rolls, I found myself sitting, still half asleep, in that early train with which I had been threatened. For some reason – I think that perhaps it was a workmen's train with cheap fares – it was crowded, so that even Holmes had not been able to secure a private compartment this time. Holmes took a seat in a corner on one side of the compartment, while I had to sit in the opposite corner at the other side, so that we had no opportunity for direct conversation. My near neighbours were country folk, a farmer and his wife who spoke in some strange patois amongst which I could barely recognize a few words with Germanic roots. They were kindly people, though, for the man gave me a fill of strong and aromatic tobacco and a tiny glass of some clear liquor which took my breath away, at which he laughed heartily and told me with much waving of arms and emphasis on words that meant nothing to me that it was *slivova*, which I knew meant home-made plum brandy. And his wife shyly handed me a huge slice of some curious game pie which more than compensated for the deficiencies of breakfast. By the time they got out at a little wayside halt, I was sorry to see them go. And, whether it was the pie or the plum brandy or the tobacco, or perhaps all three, I was feeling as fit as a fiddle by noon, when our train reached the station at Dopzhe, the ancient 'Quadrimontium' of the Romans, that for centuries had been the capital of Bohemia.

Holmes, who had been dozing in his corner seat for the last hour or so, stood up and took our bags from the rack. 'Ready, Watson?'

'Ready for anything.' Despite my boastful tone, a nagging doubt had been creeping over me for some time, and as the crowd thinned and I was able to speak more discreetly to Holmes, I muttered, 'Have you formed any plan of campaign? After all, we can hardly just march up to the palace door and demand to see the king, can we?'

Holmes smiled. 'Can we not?' And as I evidently looked unconvinced, he added, 'Remember that the king has used our services in the past. He will be forgetful and ungrateful indeed if he does not grant us the favour of a few minutes' interview.'

'I suppose that's true.' I was somewhat heartened by this, for I had been rather downcast at the thought that I had no idea as to where we might start our investigations. But what Holmes said was true, the king certainly had cause to be grateful to Holmes, and between the three of us we ought to be able to rough out some plan of action. I followed Holmes, then, with a confident stride, to the main square that lay just outside the station.

As Holmes hailed an ancient fiacre with an equally ancient horse and a driver even more ancient yet, I stood and took my first close look at the royal city of the hereditary kings of Bohemia. Of all those cities which I had visited it was perhaps most reminiscent of Paris, with wide boulevards and some impressive public buildings, almost all new or relatively so. I was to learn later that the present king's father had been greatly influenced by the French architects of his day and built, or rather rebuilt, the central area of his capital city accordingly. There were other influences too, though, for at the other side of the square the feeble spring sun was reflected in a blaze from the gold leaf that covered the dome of a mosque, a reminder that this had once been one of the farthest provinces of the Ottoman empire. Out in the countryside, as I would also learn later, the buildings were more humble, more often than not of wood, and exhibited the Turkish influence to a very marked degree.

The phrase, 'the crossroads of history,' is a hackneyed one, but it is true enough of Bohemia, for many peoples have met, fought, and settled here, Magyar and Turk, Hun and Vandal, Goth and Rus, all have left their mark. The people are as diverse as the architecture, and this diversity is nowhere more apparent than in their everyday speech, for the nobles and aristocracy speak French, the tradesmen and middle class speak German, while the country folk speak what I can only suppose is Bohemian, a dialect of Czech peculiar to the place, but with borrowings from French, German, Russian and Turkish, the last more marked in the outlying provinces.

It was not my intention to write a guide book; but this diversity was brought home to me when our driver, observing from a sidelong glance that we were two men unaccompanied by any women, suggested in hoarse German a variety of 'entertainments' for our consideration. Needless to say, we ignored him, thereby provoking a shrug of the shoulders and a muttered, 'Gospodini!' which translates as 'gentlemen,' but in a pejorative sense, as meaning 'stuck-up, toffee-nosed, and generally far too good to speak to a humble chap like me!' His attitude changed when we reached our hotel, the Albion, and I handed him a tip the modesty of which was intended to reflect his surly behaviour. He practically kissed me on both cheeks before leaping into his seat and driving off at a good pace. It was not until Holmes, with some acerbity, pointed out the peculiarities of the Bohemian currency that I realized that I had given the driver a little under five pounds sterling for a journey lasting some five minutes! It was, of course, too late to remedy matters, but I resolved to solve the mystery of the exchange rate before I parted with so much as another kopek, much less a forint or a kreuzer.

The manager of the Albion, Herr Mueller, was a Swiss. He welcomed us warmly in French, thereby paying us the compliment of thinking we were gentry. Holmes already had a good grasp of the geography of Dopzhe, gained from his guide book, and Herr Mueller confirmed that the route to the royal palace was as Holmes outlined. Herr Mueller added that the palace guards, in their ceremonial uniforms dating from great antiquity (I took it he meant the style, rather than the uniforms themselves), were a popular sight with tourists, but that it was no use our going there just at the moment, as they would all be taking their luncheon. This was said with a nod in the direction of the dining room, and Holmes, after asking that our modest luggage be taken up to our rooms, said that we would follow the guards' example, adding to me in an undertone, 'It seems that the Bohemian army shares your sense of priorities, Watson.'

'Very sensible, too,' I said. 'There's no war just at the moment, is there? Why should they – and we – not take lunch?'

At which Holmes laughed, and said that he would leave the choice of menu to me. I cannot now remember just what I elected to have, but I recall that, in common with most meals I had in Bohemia, it included some sort of potato dumpling, and that it produced a post-prandial lethargy that was not entirely unpleasant or unwelcome.

I had little time for rest, though, for as soon as we had smoked a cigarette Holmes was on his feet and looking for his hat and stick. I tried to tell him that the guards probably ate more heavily than we had done, and that very likely they had a lengthy siesta as well, but he studiously ignored the hint. I sighed, and stood up in my turn, following Holmes outside. He strode off confidently across the great square, through some narrow cobbled streets, and out into a wide boulevard. Carriages and fiacres rolled along at a stately pace, ladies and gentlemen in their finery were taking the air, and a file of lancers in ornate uniforms clattered past. Holmes nodded to the opposite side of the road, and I looked where he indicated, to see a low, long building, surrounded by a high wrought-iron fence, and with a couple of soldiers in quaint costumes on guard outside the gate.

'The palace?' I hazarded.

'Just so. Now – ah!' Holmes smiled with some satisfaction as a carriage, ordinary enough, with no coat of arms or other decoration on its exterior, swung through the gate and into the palace forecourt. The two guards showed no sign that they had even noticed its passing. A footman hurried out of the huge doorway to assist the passengers within the carriage.

Holmes said, 'We should have no difficulty reaching the door, at any rate!'

Privately I was not quite so positive. The guards on the gate most probably had their orders from the sergeant, look out for Monsieur So-and-so's carriage at such and such an hour, and allow it in without let or hindrance. But they would not have had similar orders concerning two un-known Englishmen! I had half a notion that we ought to be wearing court dress, instead of our homely tweeds; we would look out of place among the nobility, jackdaws among peacocks. Still, Holmes was a couple of paces in front of me so he, and not I, would have to face the challenge. And then, too, we came here not as scavengers but as avengers, hawks rather than jackdaws, here to do the king a good turn, if we could. I straightened my shoulders and strode out as confidently as I could manage.

I need not have worried, though. The guards never shifted as we strolled past, Holmes unconcerned, and myself a touch apprehensive. The same footman appeared as if by magic, looking very stern. In French, he asked us, 'What would Messieurs desire?'

'We would be grateful for a word with one of His Majesty's secretaries, or equerries, were that possible,' said Holmes.

The footman's face cleared. 'Of course, Monsieur. Please follow me.' And he led us through a maze of corridors and into a little ante-room, hung with tapestries and crowded with ormolu pieces. 'Messieurs have their visiting cards?' We handed them to him, and he bowed again. 'I shall not keep you a moment. If Messieurs would kindly take a seat?' and while we did that, he vanished from view.

'Easier than I thought it might be, Holmes.'

He nodded. 'I confess that I had some trepidation, Watson. But there is no reason why we should not be admitted, after all.'

'No, I suppose not.' I sank back in my comfortable armchair with some satisfaction. My luncheon, as I think I have told you, had been of the sort which is conducive to slumber, and the cushions were really very deep and soft. However, I had scarcely settled myself when there was a footstep outside and the door opened. I struggled to my feet as a middle-aged man, a touch under the average height, entered the room.

'Mr Sherlock Holmes?' He spoke in English, and as he spoke he glanced from one to the other of us.

'I am Sherlock Holmes, and this is Doctor Watson.'

'Your names are, of course, well known to me, as are your reputations, gentlemen. Forgive me, I have not introduced myself. I am the Freiherr von Kirchoff, and I have the honour to be His Majesty's private secretary.'

We exchanged bows, and Holmes said, 'It is a delicate matter upon which we are here, sir. If it were possible, we should like to speak to the king himself.'

Von Kirchoff raised an eyebrow. He said, 'You honour us with your presence, gentlemen, but at the same time you will be aware that the king has many calls upon his time, and more especially now, when there are preparations under way for a most important state visit.'

'Just so,' said Holmes.

'If I might, therefore, ask the nature of your business?'

'It is a matter of the gravest importance.'

Von Kirchoff smiled, a thin little smile. 'One would hardly expect the king to grant an audience for anything less!'

'It touches on the very safety of the kingdom.'

Von Kirchoff gave the most delicate of shrugs. 'I am, as I say, the king's private secretary.'

'Very well, since you insist upon it. It concerns one Mrs Norton, the former Miss Irene Adler.'

I was looking at von Kirchoff's face, and it was almost impassive at the mention of Miss Adler. Almost, but not quite. He told Holmes, 'If you would wait just one moment? I shall tell His Majesty you are here.' And he bowed and went out.

I sought the comfort of my armchair once again, and again I had little time to appreciate its luxury, for the door opened soundlessly and a footman appeared. Holmes and I stood up, but the footman merely smiled and said, 'If Messieurs would follow?' Naturally I expected him to turn round and lead the way out, but instead he closed the door behind him, crossed the room, and touched some hidden catch or spring in the wall, causing a section of it to slide back. The footman said, 'It is a little dark and a little damp, I fear, so if Messieurs will follow carefully, and be sure to look where they tread?' He reached into the recess behind the hidden door and took down a lamp, which he lit. Then with another little bow he stepped cautiously through the door and down a narrow stair.

'Secret passage, eh, Holmes?' I muttered as I made ready to follow.

Holmes laughed quietly. 'As found in all the best palaces, Doctor. From what we have learned, it was a necessity rather than a luxury.'

At this point the footman turned, frowned, and put finger to his lips, to indicate that we were making too much noise with our jesting. Duly admonished, we followed in silence down the narrow stair, along a passage with more than one abrupt turning, and down a second, much longer, flight of steps which ended in a door. The footman fiddled with a catch, the door swung outwards, and we found ourselves in a second corridor, this one stone-flagged and much broader than the first one we had traversed. We were evidently in the very bowels of the earth, beneath the main palace building, probably in a corridor used by the kitchen staff or something of the sort, as I judged.

The footman closed the door through which we had just

come, and I had some difficulty in seeing where it had been, so cleverly was it disguised to look like the wall of the corridor. The footman saw me stare, and permitted himself a little smile. 'It has been useful more than once, Monsieur, in the olden times. And more recently, too,' he added in an undertone.

He led us a score of paces along the corridor, stopped before a heavy oak door, produced a key and unlocked the door. 'Messieurs?' He stood aside to let us enter.

Holmes went in first, and I followed. The footman came in close on my heels, and set the lamp down on a roughly made deal table. 'If Messieurs would wait just a short while?' And with a bow he was gone, shutting the door behind him. To my utter astonishment, we then heard the key turn in the lock!

'Holmes?' I strode to the door and tried it. 'That fellow has locked us in, Holmes!'

'I had observed as much,' Holmes replied drily. He held the lamp up to illuminate the room, and I saw a couple of grimy straw mattresses on the floor, the table I had already noted, and nothing else in the way of furniture. There was no window, which did not surprise me as I already knew that we must be below ground level, but there was a sort of fanlight, with heavy iron bars, set high in the roof, which allowed a little light to penetrate. There was not enough light to provide decent illumination, but Holmes blew the lamp out none the less. 'We may need it later,' he told me, as we sat glumly on one of the mattresses and let our eyes become accustomed to what seemed like a dull twilight – and this despite the fact that my watch showed that it was a little before three in the afternoon!

I took another look around the place. 'A rum do, this, Holmes.'

'As you say, Watson.'

'Straw mattresses, you see.'

'Just so.'

'Bars on the window, and the window too high to be accessible.'

'Indeed.'

'Heavy oak door, locked from the outside.'

'Your observations are accurate in every particular. And your conclusion, Doctor?'

'Well, Holmes, if I didn't know better, I should say that we were in one of the palace dungeons!'

Holmes clapped his hands and laughed in the strange noiseless fashion that was habitual to him.

'What is not quite so easy to conjecture, though,' I went on, 'is why?'

'Ah, now there you have me, Watson.'

'And while the situation is not without its humorous aspects – we come here to do the king a good turn, and end up in the clink – it does make you wonder, does it not?'

'It does, Watson.' Holmes mused in silence for a moment. 'I can only think that the king is anxious not to have the matter made public.'

'Very sensible.'

'Still –'

'Still,' I finished for him, 'there must be more salubrious ante-rooms than this.'

'One would think so, would one not? But then if the king, or his courtiers, intended us any harm, why not shoot us out of hand?'

'Perhaps they don't want a fuss within the palace itself?' I suggested. 'These dungeons were probably part of the old palace, and have very likely witnessed more than their share of torture, and very possibly more than one discreet execution.'

'I hope you are wrong, Watson – ah!' Holmes sat up, alert, gazing at the door.

For a moment I could hear nothing, but then I detected a heavy footstep, a man striding along in boots, by the sound of it. Then a rattle as the key was inserted into the lock of the door.

Holmes and I struggled to our feet as the door opened, and a man dressed in an elaborate military uniform walked in. 'Mr Holmes? Doctor Watson?' He cursed softly. 'Is there no lamp in this damned place?'

A second man, whom I recognized as the footman who had decoyed us here, scurried into the cell and lit the lamp.

'Ah, that is better.' He bowed, and clicked his heels. 'Bertram von Gratz, gentlemen, at your service.'

Von Gratz! This, then, was that good friend of the king, and of the erstwhile Miss Adler, who had taken the famous photograph which had caused so much trouble, first to the king, then to Mrs Norton herself, and now looked likely to inconvenience the king for a second time, unless Holmes and I were able to prevent it. Von Gratz was a handsome enough man, the sort of man who looks younger than the calendar would convey, tall and broad-shouldered, with dark curly hair and black eyes which regarded us keenly.

'I am Sherlock Holmes, and this is Doctor Watson.'

'An honour, sir.' Von Gratz stepped further into the cell, and told the footman, 'Leave us.'

'Very good, Herr Oberst-Baron.' He went out, closing the door but leaving it unlocked.

Von Gratz smiled without humour. 'I should tell you that there are two armed guards outside,' he said in an offhand manner. 'Now, Mr Holmes, I must ask you what is this nonsense about the king and Miss Adler? Or Mrs Norton, as I understand she is now?'

Holmes frowned. 'The king has told you nothing?'

'About what?'

'I understood you were a good friend of His Majesty?'

Von Gratz put a hand on the hilt of his sword. 'I have that honour, sir,' he said stiffly.

'H'mm. His Majesty would tell you if there had been any threat?'

'What sort of threat?'

In a few words, Holmes outlined the situation as we knew it. When he mentioned the photograph, von Gratz's stern expression softened, only to grow thunderous when Holmes mentioned Karl, the king's illegitimate half-brother. And when Holmes explained that Karl had stolen the Adler papers and proposed to use them to force the king's abdication, von Gratz made fluent use of the lower sort of German expressions, employing some words and phrases which were entirely new to me, but which I mentally noted for future use. When he had exhausted his extensive vocabulary, he struck the table top with his open hand. 'But there has been no threat of any sort, not up to now,' he told us. 'I can swear to that.'

'Mrs Norton did think that Karl and his confederate, Gottfried, would keep the photograph back until the last minute,' I reminded Holmes.

Von Gratz nodded. 'Yes, that makes sense. If they were to show their hand too soon, then we – the king, I mean, and his loyal friends – could make plans accordingly.' He glanced around the room, as if seeing it for the first time, and roared with laughter. 'I should have apologized for these sordid surroundings, gentlemen, but when I was told who you were, and heard something of why you were here, I thought that perhaps –' and he broke off in evident embarrassment.

'You thought that perhaps we proposed a little blackmail on our own account?' suggested Holmes.

'No! That is – well, Mr Holmes, I knew that you were privy to the king's most secret business, and I knew nothing of Mrs Norton's troubles, Karl's theft of the photograph, and so forth. So I naturally thought that discretion was indicated. And now you have confirmed that I was right. I may have misjudged you, gentlemen, but I can at least claim some small credit for spotting the danger to the king.' He laughed, then grew serious. 'If I might prevail upon you to remain here just a short while more? I shall not lock you in this time, I assure you, but the fewer people who know you are here, the better. I must tell His Majesty what you have told me, then the four of us can meet in more select surroundings and make our plans together.' He clicked his heels, bowed, and left. We heard him shouting orders in the corridor, and a moment later our old friend the footman rushed in, followed by a half dozen of his fellows, with chairs, a huge candelabrum, and a box of fine cigars.

We smoked in silence for a time, then I heard the heavy footsteps of von Gratz in the corridor. Holmes and I stood up as the door opened.

'Gentlemen, my apologies for keeping you here,' said von Gratz. 'If you would follow me?' and he led us into the corridor, stopping at the same concealed door by which we had originally come here. 'A hackneyed device, I fear,' he said with a laugh, 'but useful enough under the circumstances.' He lit a lamp, and led us up the stairs, along a maze of narrow passages, dusty and cobwebby, to what I took to be another secret door. He touched the latch, and we stepped out into a large, well-lit room, blinking as the light struck our eyes, which had grown accustomed to the dimness of the nether regions.

As we stepped through the concealed door, a tall man rose from the desk at which he had been seated, and held out a hand to us. 'Mr Holmes! Doctor! Please sit down, and have a cigar.'

And I found myself shaking the hand of His Majesty Wilhelm Gottsreich Sigismond von Ormstein, Grand Duke of Cassel-Felstein, Count and Elector of the Holy Roman Empire, Grand Master of the Order of Saint Wenceslas and of the Order of Saint Hugh of Grenoble, and hereditary King of Bohemia.

FOUR

The king lit a cigar, stared at it in silence for a while, then threw it away with an exclamation of disgust. He then made some remarks, addressed to no-one in particular, and neither temperate nor brief in duration, regarding the villainous Karl.

When the king eventually paused for breath, Holmes said, 'All that Your Majesty says concerning your half-brother may well be true –'

'Particularly regarding his parentage!' I muttered.

'– but it hardly gets us anywhere,' Holmes went on.

The king smiled. 'You are right, of course, Mr Holmes, but I could not have given my full attention to the problem until I had got that off my chest, as they say. I assure you that there will be no further outburst of that sort.'

'I am glad to hear Your Majesty say so.' Holmes frowned. 'You say that Karl and Gottfried have not yet shown their hand?'

The king shook his head. 'There have been no threats, or anything of that kind.'

'It occurs to me,' I put in, 'that we may have been precipitate in coming here at all. Possibly Karl is still in Paris, and the photograph with him?'

Holmes was silent for a moment, then said, 'Your Majesty?'

The king shrugged his shoulders. 'Bertie?'

Von Gratz said, 'I imagine that Karl will want to seek the protection of Gottfried's schloss as soon as possible. Paris is too dangerous, the criminal underworld holds men who, for a very few francs, would slit Karl's throat for us. For anyone who would pay them, that is,' he added, with a grim smile. 'And another point is that Gottfried would wish for Karl, and the photograph, to be where he – Gottfried, I mean – can keep an eye on them.'

'Oh?' said Holmes quickly. 'Is there some difference there, then? If so, might we not make use of that?'

'It is what in English you would call "six of one and half a dozen of the other", I think,' said von Gratz. 'They need one another, for Karl can hope for nothing on his own account; it is Gottfried who has some claim to the throne –'

Here the king snorted loudly, as if to dispute the last statement.

'In his own opinion, sire,' said von Gratz rather hastily.

'Just so,' said the king, mollified.

'You were saying –?' said Holmes, with a touch of impatience.

'Ah, yes. Karl, I say, needs Gottfried,' von Gratz went on, 'but then Gottfried is no hardened villain, no man of action. He needs Karl to do his dirty work for him. An uneasy truce, as you might say.'

I asked, 'Could Your Majesty not simply arrest Karl? I understood that he had undertaken to leave Bohemia, never to return?'

The king frowned. 'That arrangement was purely informal, between Karl and my late father,' said he. 'There is nothing in writing, nothing a judge would act upon, and Karl has, to outward appearance at least, committed no crime.'

'And we do not even know for certain that he is here.

Would there be any way of determining whether Karl has in fact entered Bohemia?' asked Holmes, with no real conviction in his voice that such would prove to be the case. 'You have police, customs officials?'

Von Gratz shook his head. 'The customs examination, as doubtless you know at first hand, is concerned with tobacco and spirits only. There is no need for visitors to show a passport, and even if there were any enquiry, Karl is quite capable of producing forged papers. Unless he were to use his real name, we cannot hope to tell if he is here in the country or not.'

'I see,' said Holmes.

There was a silence, broken only by the king's saying, half to himself, 'I could almost sympathize with Karl. He is my half-brother, when all is said and done. My father made him a generous allowance, did you know that? I only found out months after my father's death, when the allowance had ceased, of course. I tried to contact Karl, to make some amends, perhaps offer to continue the payments. Extend the hand of friendship at the very least. But my agents could not trace him, he had moved house. He has, perhaps, reason to be angry. The merest accident of birth –' and he shrugged his shoulders and relapsed into a moody silence.

I could see what he meant, to some extent. Only the absence of a wedding ring, a certificate, prevented Karl from being king. On the other hand, I had seen many a man – and woman, too – in the poorer districts of London, who had not even those advantages which Karl had inherited, and who had made their way honestly, without railing at their parents, or at fate, because they had not been born with the proverbial silver spoon in their mouths.

The king broke the silence again. 'I must apologize for

your offhand treatment,' he told us, 'but I could not be sure that your intentions were honourable. You are aware of the situation, yes? Then you will understand that just at the moment I am perhaps a trifle susceptible to fears and fancies. Again, I apologize for my unworthy suspicions of you.'

'Fears, fancies and suspicions not altogether without foundation, I must say,' said Holmes, 'though Your Majesty failed to identify the true source of those fears, et cetera.'

The king managed a smile. 'True, and I should have known from which quarter the threat would come.'

Holmes nodded. 'To sum it up, then, we think that Karl will have entered Bohemia undetected, unsuspected, and that he is now in Gottfried's castle?'

The king and von Gratz nodded agreement.

'And the photograph?' Holmes continued. 'Will that be in the castle, or elsewhere?'

'The castle,' said von Gratz. 'They would wish to know that it was where they can lay hands on it instantly.'

'I agree,' said the king.

'Very well,' said Holmes. 'The problem thus resolves itself into how to enter the castle and recover the photograph.'

Von Gratz laughed aloud, and even the king permitted a smile to enliven his dour features. 'You put it simply, Mr Holmes,' said von Gratz, 'but it will not be quite so easy as you make it sound. Schloss Württemburg is well-nigh impregnable, proof against all but a prolonged siege.'

'And moreover,' added the king, 'we – I – dare not be seen using the army against Gottfried. For one thing, questions, awkward questions, would be asked. And for another, Gottfried's supporters would very likely take up arms on his behalf.'

Holmes frowned. 'I was given to understand that the army is loyal to Your Majesty?'

'It is,' said the king. 'But the army, however loyal, is only small. Excellent fellows, every one of them, and they would fight to the death for me, for Bohemia, or for the honour of their regiments, but loyalty and bravery cannot replace sheer force of numbers. Faced with the armies of our neighbours, Prussia, let us say, or our cousin the Tsar's Cossacks – well! As I said, it would be to the death, no doubt of that; but equally there is no doubt as to who the victors would be.'

'Even so,' said Holmes, 'what forces could Gottfried field against a loyal and determined army, even if its numbers are not great?'

'The business classes,' said the king. 'Gottfried has led a blameless life – unlike myself! You must understand that the political situation in my country is a very delicate balance of power between internal factions. The army depends for its funds upon taxes, that is to say upon the merchant class, who in turn rely upon the army for protection from covetous neighbouring powers. Gottfried appeals strongly to the merchants and lawyers, who see his outlook as mirroring their own. If those men were to witness what would seem to be military action against a Bohemian nobleman who had committed no crime, and a nobleman with whom they so closely sympathize, they would be very inclined to be troublesome. Possibly they would even invite one of our neighbouring countries to send its armies into Bohemia to "restore order", as the convenient diplomatic phrase has it. An invitation which some of our neighbours would not hesitate to accept, I might add.'

'And as a further consideration,' added von Gratz, 'if

there were any unrest, we might expect some trouble from those anarchists and nihilists who have recently been active across Europe.'

'And here?' asked Holmes quickly.

Von Gratz shook his head. 'Nothing to speak of as yet, thank Heaven! We arrested one misguided young man, a student at the university here in Dopzhe, who attacked the Prime Minister with a knife three months ago. And a workman threw a bomb at the royal carriage last year, but without doing any harm, the bomb failed to go off and the anarchist was shot by the guards. But there have been pamphlets, posters on the walls of public buildings, the customary prelude to civil unrest.'

'H'mm. I had not realized that the political situation was quite so complex,' said Holmes.

Personally, I thought this something of an understate-ment. If Holmes and I were to tackle not only the king's half-brother, and Duke Gottfried, and the massed shop-keepers of Bohemia, but also sundry anarchists wielding knives and bombs, *and* we could not even rely upon the support of the army, then it rather looked as if we should have our work cut out! Pointless saying as much, of course, so I tried to look as wise as I might under the circum-stances.

Holmes thought in silence for a moment, all eyes upon him. Then he slapped his hands down on his knees, as if he had come to a decision, and stood up. 'If it is not to be by force of arms, then it must be by stealth,' he told us. 'I confess that I am not altogether unhappy at the prospect, for I always think that I work better alone, and best of all with Watson by my side. I shall, however, need someone with local knowledge, were that possible.'

'Bertie?' said the king.

Von Gratz stood up and clicked his heels. 'It will be an honour to work with the celebrated Sherlock Holmes,' said he. 'I have known the area well, since I was a boy.'

'And you may rely upon me in all respects,' said the king. 'All, that is, save one. I cannot appear in this matter at all. The cavalier treatment meted out to you just now, the delicate situation I have outlined – one was a symptom, the other the cause, of my distress.' He put a hand to his brow. 'I dare not be seen to be employing an agent, much less a foreign agent. I dare not be seen to be acting against my own cousin, much less my half-brother. Above all, I must avoid any suspicion, any breath of scandal, at least for the next year until the treaty is signed with the King of Scandinavia.'

'I understand perfectly, Your Majesty,' said Holmes with a bow.

So did I. All the oft-repeated apologies, all the detailed explanations, boiled down to the plain fact that we were on our own. If we failed, we should take the blame for the ruin of the king, and Bohemia along with him, while if we succeeded, we should get no praise. And if we were discovered, the king would throw us to the wolves! I bowed in my turn, took the prescribed three steps backwards, and started to follow Holmes to the door.

'A moment, gentlemen,' said von Gratz. 'With your permission, sire?' And he sought the secret panel, opened it, and took the lamp from its hook just inside the concealed passage. 'A necessary precaution,' he told us with a smile, before bowing to the king and leading the way through the opening in the wall.

We followed him through the maze of corridors, until he opened another door and we emerged into a plainly furnished sitting room. 'My own humble quarters,' von Gratz told us. He waved us to chairs and handed us his cigar case. 'A brandy and soda? No? In that case, we had best get down to business. Mr Holmes, you said that we must effect an entrance to Schloss Württemburg by stealth, rather than direct attack, and we all agree as to that. I must now ask, have you formed any plan of campaign?'

'Not as yet,' Holmes was forced to admit. 'I was hoping that you could tell me something more of Gottfried and his castle, some information that might perhaps be of use to us?'

Von Gratz considered the end of his cigar carefully. 'Where to start?' he mused.

'Start with the name,' I suggested. 'I had thought that Württemburg was much further west, in Germany?'

'Ah, you are thinking of the province of Baden-Württemburg, perhaps?' said von Gratz. 'No connection at all, Doctor. Our historians have postulated that there may have been some historical link between the two places, and I believe that the university here has awarded several doctorates to internationally noted scholars for research on the matter, but no real conclusion has ever been reached.'

'More or less par for the course, there. And the castle itself?'

'The castle itself is situated close to the village of Kleinwald. The hamlet, rather, for the place is, as its name might suggest, tiny, and set among the forests. The castle is set on a rocky outcrop with only one practicable approach, that which leads from the village up a fairly steep slope to the main gate.'

'No possibility of entering by a back window or anything of the kind?' asked Holmes.

Von Gratz shook his head. 'The cliffs might be negotiated

by a chamois or ibex,' he told us, 'or indeed by a determined and expert climber, though I should not care to make the experiment myself. But then the windows are generally of that very traditional type depicted in children's picture books, that is they are no more than slits high up in the walls. Later occupants have, it is true, added more modern windows here and there, but they have stout shutters, besides being inaccessible.'

'H'mm. No possibility of there being a secret passage, I suppose?' asked Holmes with a smile and a glance at the secret panel by which we had entered this very room.

'An ancient place like that, I dare say there are a dozen,' answered von Gratz carelessly. 'But if so, then they are so secret that I do not know them!'

'Any sign on the door, "No hawkers, no circulars", though?' I asked.

Von Gratz stared at me.

I went on, 'There must be visitors, tradesmen, calling at the castle, surely? Could we not pose as itinerant onion sellers or something of the sort?'

Von Gratz laughed, then nodded. 'Not exactly onion sellers, perhaps,' he said, 'but, yes. On my own visits to Schloss Württemburg, when I was a very small boy, I recollect seeing the tradesmen's carts toiling up the ramp to the main gate, and the butler and cooks turning out to greet them. The place is so isolated, you understand, that any human contact is welcomed by the staff there.'

Holmes sat up. 'Ah, so you have been inside the castle itself, then?'

Von Gratz nodded. 'The old duke had no children of his own, and the king and myself used to visit him frequently in the school holidays.'

'That may prove useful,' said Holmes. 'Are you also acquainted with Gottfried?'

Von Gratz shook his head. 'When the old duke died, the title and lands passed to his nearest relative, a distant cousin of the duke. That was Gottfried's father, and when he died in turn, a year or so after coming into the title, then Gottfried became duke. Up until then, I had never met Gottfried. And frankly, from what I have seen of him since he inherited, I was not missing much. I have not visited the castle since the old duke died, which would be ten – no, twelve – years ago.'

'H'mm. But the plans of the castle will not have changed since then, I expect, so it will still be useful. And the tradesmen of whom you spoke, they come from the village?'

'Hardly. It is too small a place to boast anything but a small and rather grimy beer house. The farmers and so on grow their own vegetables, of course, but the other necessities come from the town of Marienburg, three miles or so to the south. The country folk in these outlying provinces seldom visit a town, much less a city. The farmers, perhaps, go to a fair once a month or so, and the others, if they can walk or borrow a horse, might visit the town on a great feast day, but the older folk, and the women and children, seldom stir far from where they were born. The tradesmen tour the villages and hamlets, you understand, two or three times each week, taking their wares to the people, and not the other way round. Yes, and once or twice each week, they would visit the schloss.' Von Gratz looked eagerly at Holmes. 'You think there may be possibilities there?'

'It seems that Watson's suggestion is the only one likely to have the remotest chance of success.'

I basked for a brief moment in the unaccustomed luxury of the praise, but frankly the more I thought about the scheme, the more madcap it seemed to me. 'Granted that we might gain entry to the castle courtyard,' I said, 'we are unlikely to get further than the kitchens without being challenged.'

Holmes waved this aside. 'We must take one step at a time,' he said. 'Our first task is to gain entry, if only to the courtyard as you put it.'

We arranged that Holmes and I should remain at the Hotel Albion that night, and that von Gratz would collect us early next morning, and then we should all travel together to Marienburg, there to develop our scheme as much as we might after first-hand observation of the practical aspects.

Von Gratz took us to one of the reception rooms, then called a footman to see us out, saying that it would be as well if we were not seen together too much, as even now we could not be certain that Gottfried and Karl did not have their spies within the court itself. 'Indeed,' said von Gratz carelessly, 'I should be most surprised if they did not, for it is a logical course of action.' Which may have been perfectly true, but it did little to cheer me up.

Holmes spent most of the evening smoking in silence, and I must confess that I too had some hard thinking to do. Not for the first time, my association with Holmes was leading me from my safe harbour into waters that were not merely deep and murky but positively dangerous to boot. True, I was a willing volunteer, not a reluctant conscript; but even so, it behoved me, if only for the sake of my dear wife, to minimize the risks if I could. In particular, it seemed to me that however difficult it might prove to enter our enemies' lair, it would probably prove a jolly sight more difficult to get out again! I have already noted that when we first came into the ancient forest lands I found myself recalling the old fairy tales, myths and legends. The fable that now came irresistibly to my mind was that of Rapunzel, sitting in her high tower, with a window opening to the outside world, but no means of using that window, for either ingress or egress. Such was the unenviable position that we should find ourselves in, were we to find the great gate of the castle closed against us, and ourselves on the inside. I came to a couple of conclusions, both fairly obvious; one of them was to write to Mary, to assure her that I was thinking of her, and was in no sort of danger – I hoped that would not prove to have been wishful thinking! – and I accordingly found pen and paper and composed a few sentences along those lines, before turning in and spending a very restless night.

Von Gratz arrived promptly next morning as we were finishing breakfast. He had changed his army uniform for a suit of that dull green woollen cloth called 'loden', which is much favoured by huntsmen and country folk in Germany and the surrounding lands, with a cloak of the same material. Holmes and I had our tweed suits, respectable enough for company, but not so stylish as to attract too much attention in rustic parts. All in all, we looked like three men of the middle class who had decided to take a walking holiday in the forest, and that would be sufficient disguise for the present.

We caught a train, no express this, but a little train that took folk from the capital to the spa and hotel towns in the north of Bohemia, and I think made its way slowly across country to Danzig, in due course. An hour or so later, and we were in the old town of Marienburg, which bears an air of faded grandeur. Once a fashionable watering place – there is still a hint of sulphur in the air when the wind is in a certain direction – it has been overtaken by Baden-Baden and the Swiss resorts, but still attracts a considerable number of visitors, largely from within Bohemia itself.

Von Gratz allowed us no time for sightseeing, though, leading us away from the once-fashionable squares near the railway station, and into streets that had pretty clearly never held any great attraction for the visitor, even when the town was in its heyday. He led us to a tiny hotel with a grandiose name, the Grand-Hôtel Royal St Georges, painted in faded gold over the narrow door.

'It is a touch run-down,' von Gratz admitted, pausing outside the door, 'but it will serve us as a temporary head-quarters. I know the place, for I had some interesting times here when I was a young man. Interesting times and interesting companions,' and he coughed ostentatiously and coloured slightly, as a man in his thirties does when he thinks of the follies of his twenties. Without further reminiscence he led us inside, and booked a suite of rooms without difficulty, for the place was empty save for a couple of commercial travellers. The proprietor was a young man whom von Gratz did not recognize – it transpired that the hotel had changed hands more than once in the last couple of years as its fortunes declined – but he knew the town well, and when von Gratz enquired 'Was Signor Tommaso Valentini still in business selling Italian specialities?' the proprietor nodded, but without enthusiasm.

'His shop is still in the centre of town,' he told us, 'but his prices are a trifle steep for the likes of me. I buy just as good in the old market, when it gets near to closing and they are desperate to get rid of their surplus. Will the gentlemen be taking dinner here?'

We declined the offer, and took our own bags up to our rooms. Holmes asked, 'Surely an exclusive purveyor of imported delicacies cannot expect to sell any great quantity to the ordinary country folk?'

Von Gratz shook his head with a smile. 'No, that is true. But old Tommaso used to deliver to the castle two or three times a week. I am hoping he still does so. Or, if not, that he can tell us who does still deliver out that way. Besides, it is as well that this fellow downstairs thinks we are looking to buy pasta or Parmesan cheese, rather than that he suspects our true purpose.'

Holmes nodded. 'If you are not too fatigued by the journey, we might make some preliminary enquiry now,' said he. He glanced at me and smiled. 'If nothing else, we might make a respectable luncheon with some bread, cheese, olives and Italian country wine.'

'I must say, Holmes, I don't know why you look at me when you say that!' I told him. 'Still, it is almost the hour when one starts to think of luncheon, now that you mention it.'

Von Gratz took us back into the more fashionable part of the town, past little jewellers' and furriers' shops, their windows set out neatly enough, but all bearing that same air of faded glory that characterized the whole town; the displays were not dusty, exactly, but they all looked as if they had last been rearranged twenty years or so ago. We stopped before a little shop, which bore the name 'Valentini', and a legend which advertised all manner of imported merchandise, sweet and savoury.

We went inside, and a young man of distinctly Mediterranean aspect came forward and bowed. 'Sirs?'

'Your pardon, sir,' said von Gratz, 'it was Signor Valentini that I sought.'

Another bow. 'At your service, sir.'

'Ah, it was Signor Tommaso Valentini.'

The young man smiled. 'My uncle, sir. He is in the back room.' He turned and looked back at von Gratz. 'Begging the gentleman's pardon, but I have the feeling that we have met?'

'We have indeed,' said von Gratz. 'I am Bertram von Gratz, and you are Luigi, are you not? I last saw you twenty years back, when we were about fifteen years old. We wrestled for the hand of a young lady – Emmelina, was it?'

'Esmeralda,' said the young man with a broad grin. 'I won, I recall!'

'True,' said von Gratz. 'What happened to Esmeralda, do you know?'

'I married her! One moment, and I shall call my uncle,' and off he went, to return a very short time later with a little old man, who grinned broadly as he saw von Gratz.

There were the usual reminiscences and handshakes, the inevitable photographs of the wife and of three fine children, before we got down to business. 'Tell me,' said von Gratz, 'do you still deal with the folk at the Schloss Württemburg?'

The old man nodded. 'As a matter of fact, we have an order from the kitchens now,' he said. 'To be delivered the day after tomorrow.'

'Ah! In that case,' said von Gratz, 'I should like to beg a favour – no, two favours. One, that the delivery might be advanced by a day, to tomorrow; and two, that we three might take charge of it. How would that suit you, old friend?'

Old Tommaso frowned, then smiled. 'Ah, I have it! A prank, a joke, is that is, young sir?'

'Just so,' said von Gratz carelessly. 'A practical joke, and if anyone asks, you will tell them as much. Well, how say you?'

'Well, the delivery might be made a day early, and nobody will complain. If it were a day late, of course, that would have been different! And I know you well enough to trust you, sir, and these two gentlemen. Only, I have a couple of other orders to deliver out that way – could I rely on you for that?'

'My word on it,' said von Gratz. 'And, to make the jest better, we shall need to borrow aprons, or whatever you call them.'

Old Tommaso, entering into the spirit of the thing, took us into the storeroom behind the shop, and outfitted us each with a brown dustcoat. I took special care to ensure that mine was a good deal too big, and when Holmes looked askance I told him, 'Nobody expects a carter's coat to fit, Holmes!' with which he had to be satisfied.

After a further half hour or so of recollecting the old days, in which Holmes and I could take no part, von Gratz took his leave of the uncle and nephew, saying that we should return early the next day to receive our instructions and collect the cart. Luncheon was now very definitely indicated, and we set off for an unpretentious restaurant away from the main thoroughfare. We still wanted to be as inconspicuous as possible, for there was always a chance that someone might remember von Gratz, just as the Valentinis had done, and whilst we had every right to be there, we thought it as well that as few people as possible knew of our presence.

Our way took us through the poorer quarters of the town, and I noticed a shop catering for walkers and climbers, with a window full of rock-axes, boots and the like. Atop these was a range of those little green hats, each with what looked like a garishly coloured shaving brush in the side of it, that you see in those parts. Now, I had always had a secret fancy to have one of those hats, but never dared to indulge my fancy in London. But here it was a different matter, I should not be looking at all out of place, but merely blending in, following the local customs. I said as much to Holmes and von Gratz; I think von Gratz understood, or perhaps he had just seen enough men wearing these hats that it was no great matter to him, and Holmes merely looked very superior and said he preferred to wait outside. I went in alone, and bought the hat and a few other bits and pieces.

When I returned to the street, Holmes and von Gratz were looking in the window of a second-hand clothing shop a few doors along. I joined them, and followed Holmes's gaze to see a display of clothing that might suit a farmer's wife in the forest regions. Holmes labours under the ridiculous misapprehension that women's clothing makes an effective disguise – ridiculous because frankly he has neither the face nor the figure to carry it off – and I asked, 'Thinking of a more elaborate costume, perhaps, Holmes?'

He laughed. 'Not for myself, Watson. But it occurs to me that someone at the castle may possibly recognize our friend von Gratz.' And to von Gratz he said, 'How would you feel about dressing as a country woman?'

Von Gratz tersely indicated that he found the very notion offensive, but agreed that there was an outside chance that he might happen on someone who remembered him. After some discussion he allowed Holmes to furnish him with a broad-brimmed straw hat and a grubby scarf.

'That should suffice,' said Holmes. 'That, and Watson's new hat – which, by the way, we have not yet seen,' and he looked pointedly at my brown paper parcels.

I took out the hat and clapped it on my head. Holmes

said nothing, but merely turned and walked off at a great pace. To punish this incivility I caught up with him, linked my arm in his, and kept the hat on until we reached the restaurant, bowing as I went to the mystified passers-by. Holmes sometimes has to be put in his place.

When we had eaten, we returned to our hotel, and in our little sitting room Holmes asked von Gratz to draw a rough plan of the castle, and tell us what he recalled of it. From what I gathered, it was pretty much like the ordinary run of castles, massive, draughty and the devil's own job to keep warm. The only piece of information that seemed likely to prove at all useful was the arrangement of the old duke's own rooms, bedroom, sitting room, a small library and an even smaller 'cabinet of curiosities', a kind of miniature museum which some old duke had begun a century or more ago. These, said von Gratz, were the best rooms in the entire castle, and it seemed likely both that Gottfried would have retained them for his own use, and that the papers which we sought would be hidden in one of these rooms. Holmes concurred, and took careful note of the plans of this part of the castle, as drawn by von Gratz.

I tried to sound out Holmes as to his plan of campaign, but he only shook his head. 'Until we can see the inside of the place for ourselves, we can make no plan,' he said, and I knew from his tone that he was as dissatisfied as I was myself. The only suggestion he could advance was that once we were inside, von Gratz and I should unload the cart, whilst Holmes himself discarded his dustcoat and tried to make a search. Von Gratz pointed out that he, and not Holmes, had actually seen the inside of the castle, and that it should logically be von Gratz who left Holmes and me in the courtyard. The discussion of this point continued throughout dinner, for Holmes and von Gratz were equally stubborn. We eventually decided that we should all three stick together, sinking or swimming as we might.

We rose early next day, and made our way to the Valentinis' shop, where we collected our dustcoats. Holmes stared at my own generously tailored garment, saying, 'Much too large!'

'It won't be when I've done,' I assured him, and took myself off into a back room to change, emerging a trifle self-consciously five minutes later.

Holmes stared again. 'Watson, I congratulate you! You look two stones heavier.'

'Merely a little padding,' I told him. 'An elementary disguise, Holmes. I never yet saw a skinny carter!' and I patted my stomach like an incompetent amateur actor playing Falstaff.

We set off on our rounds. Although Schloss Württemburg was our final goal, we had undertaken to make deliveries to three other houses situated in the same general vicinity, and since we thought it likely that we should be fully occupied once we reached the duke's residence, we also thought it as well to discharge those obligations first. We called accordingly at the three houses, which as one might expect were all more substantial than the ordinary run of cottages, and at each we were received kindly by the cooks and what have you. Indeed, at one house the butler, a man of portly aspect and cheerful mien, eyed my stomach, nodded and smiled, then treated me to a foaming glass of the local beer, not unlike the Pilsner of Czechoslovakia but with something of a metallic taste to it, which my new friend told me in a hoarse whisper was not only good for my digestion but would do wonders for my marriage as well. I made a discreet note of the brand and resolved to ask my wine merchant to import a few cases.

More to the immediate purpose, at none of these houses were we regarded at all suspiciously, or treated with anything other than kindliness. As they had expected old Valentini, or his usual men, we were called upon to give some account of why we were making the delivery in each case, but we answered that we had just been hired by the shop, and this was accepted without further ado. This circumstance cheered us considerably, as seeming to show that we had nothing to fear – at least at the outset!

. Our duty done, we headed through the forests, turned a corner, and caught our first glimpse of Schloss Württemburg. The castle stood on a high, sheer-sided outcrop of rock, which had the appearance of being the central portion of an old volcano, although I cannot say whether in fact it was. It seemed to brood over the tiny village of Kleinwald, which was nothing more than a dozen little cottages scattered at the base of the outcrop. The road on which we were travelling led through the village, and then continued on and up as a steep slope, whether man-made or natural I could not tell, which made two sharp turns as it led to the great gate of the castle. It was for all the world like an illustration in a child's book of fairy tales, and under different circumstances I could have stood there and admired the prospect it provided. As it was, when I reflected that our enemies were within those massive stone walls, and that we ourselves might have a considerable task to escape unscathed, it suddenly seemed less of a fairy tale castle, and more the abode of wizards and demons, less a picture from a child's reader, more an engraving from some old and foul work of necromancy. I became aware of the forests from which we had just emerged, the oppressive gloom of the trees, the odd little sounds that you could not identify. At that moment a cloud passed across the feeble sun, and I shivered involuntarily.

'Ready, Watson?' murmured Holmes.

'Oh, I'm ready enough! I just hope you are!' I answered, throwing off all my fancies with a shrug of the shoulders.

We went through the village, answering the waves and shouts of greeting as we did so, and started up the great ramp that led to the castle gate. I am disposed to think that it must have been man-made, in part at any rate, for it was perfectly adapted to the defence of the castle. I have said that it made two sharp turns, so that you started off upwards in the direction of the castle but fifty yards to the left of the gate, then turned through ninety degrees to the right, at which point you must negotiate those fifty yards of a centre section at right angles to the gate, then another ninety-degree turn brought you to the third, last, and steepest section that led to the gate itself. It was obviously the centre section that was most dangerous, for anyone moving along that elevated causeway must present a broadside target to those in the castle. Any competent archer could pick off would-be invaders at leisure; and for a man with a repeating rifle it would be like shooting fish in a barrel! I shivered a second time, with more material cause this time.

There came no arrows, or bullets, though, as we steered the heavy cart slowly along the slope, and through the open gate into the castle courtyard. A tall fellow in a greasy apron greeted us, asking 'From old Tommaso?' and when we answered yes, he did not ask the usual question but shrugged and jerked a thumb towards the opposite side of the yard in a surly fashion. We took the cart to an open doorway that gave on to a large store room. The man who had spoken to us was nowhere to be seen, evidently thinking that it was no part of his duties to help us unload the cart. More, the courtyard was empty, and so was the store room! Holmes glanced round, then nodded to us.

'We seem to have the place to ourselves, for the moment,' he said. 'It would be remiss of us not to seize the opportunity,' and off he went, through the store room, through the door at the other side, and into a corridor. Here he stopped, and looked at von Gratz. 'Which way?'

Von Gratz looked about him, as if to get his bearings, then led the way along the corridor, up the back stairs, and through a baize door into a broader stone-flagged gallery. 'Now –' and he paused, as there was a clatter of footsteps and the sound of voices in animated discussion.

'This way!' said Holmes, in an undertone, pulling me by the arm into a dark recess. Von Gratz followed, and Holmes whispered, 'With luck, they will be off downstairs, and we can go on our way.'

The footsteps halted, but the conversation continued, evidently the men whom we could hear had paused nearby, but we could not see them. From the recess or alcove in which we sheltered I could see only a small section of corridor, and that was empty. No! To my horror, a man in livery was coming towards us. I shrank back, trying to convey to Holmes and von Gratz that we were in danger of being discovered. The footman, for such he clearly was, passed me, no more than a foot away, and I heaved a sigh of relief. Then I gasped, for he had turned, and was staring right at me!

I stood there, struck dumb, wondering what on earth to do. The footman put a finger to his lips – though he had no need to warn me to keep silent! – and whispered, 'Friends of the king?' I nodded, yes, and he went on, 'Wait!' He turned again, and disappeared from my view. I heard the voices pause, then resume as the heavy footsteps seemed to be moving away, down a flight of stone stairs if I were not mistaken.

Then there was silence. Behind me, Holmes asked, 'Watson? What happened?' but before I could make any answer the footman appeared, silently.

Holmes tensed, but I said, 'He's a friend!' and looked a question.

'This way, but quickly, and silently,' the footman told us. He led us along the corridor, up a shallow stair of three or four steps, and threw open a door. 'If the gentlemen will wait here?' and he stood aside to let us pass. 'And please be quiet, for there is much danger.'

I went in first, and Holmes and von Gratz followed. I turned, asked, 'But what –' but the footman had closed the door after us, and I heard the key turned from the outside.

I stepped back and took a better look round the room. It was bare, and there was a heavy wooden shutter over the window. I said, 'Well, this could be merely a safe haven, and that footman could be genuine. But I rather fancy that things are otherwise, and that being locked up is fast becoming a habit with us. Indeed, my next book may well be a monograph upon the dungeons and prisons of Bohemia!'

FIVE

'I blame myself,' said Holmes bitterly. 'It was, of course, too easy from the outset, too obvious. The lack of activity in the courtyard and store rooms, the loyal and obliging footman. My only excuse, if any excuse there be, it is that it was so blatant as to be incredible.' And he shook his head.

'Still, Holmes, we wanted to get into the castle, and here we are!' I told him.

He regarded me with a certain amount of contempt. 'Perfectly correct, up to a point,' said he. 'But even if we could get out of this room, I fancy that our birds will prove to have flown.'

'It is true,' said von Gratz. 'We were clearly expected, for this elaborate charade took time to prepare. As Mr Holmes says, Gottfried and Karl will be making their escape now, if they have not already done so, and the papers along with them.'

'You did say that you suspected that there might be a spy in the palace,' I reminded him.

Von Gratz nodded. 'And we now know that spy's identity, for, apart from myself, only von Kirchoff knew the business which brought you to Bohemia.'

'What, the king's private secretary?' I asked.

Von Gratz shrugged. 'Von Kirchoff is an ambitious man.

And then who is better placed to know the king's private affairs?'

'It makes sense,' said Holmes. 'Indeed, now that we know the identity of the spy, we might be able to make use of that knowledge. Or should I say, "we might have been able" to use it, for our immediate concern must be to escape from here.' He tested the door, and shook his head. 'Nothing there, I fear.'

'The shutter is not locked, though,' I said carelessly. This was true; the shutter, though stout enough, was not primarily intended either to keep prisoners in or to keep intruders out. The window's situation, high above the ground, was sufficient for that.

I ignored Holmes's look of irritation, and threw the shutters open. The window was of thick glass, criss-crossed with lead and with a coat of arms in stained glass in its centre; but the fastening was just the usual sort, and I opened that as well, and stared down at the sheer drop. The window was perhaps twenty feet up from the base of the castle's wall, and then the wall itself was built on the very edge of the rocky projection, which was perhaps some hundred feet high. The total distance to terra firma was thus around a hundred and twenty feet, all more or less vertical.

I stepped back and surveyed the window frame, solid oak, with a stout vertical wooden pillar – I don't know the right architectural term for it – in the centre of the opening. To the right of the window a heavy and ornate iron bracket, evidently to hold a torch or candles, was bolted into the stone wall.

'Now,' I said, 'if there were a bed in the room, we could tear the sheets into strips to fashion a rope. One end goes round the window post there, fastened to the iron sconce for extra safety, and the other end dangles out of the window, enabling us to scramble down.'

'True,' said Holmes, with every appearance of sincerity. 'And if we had a hot-air balloon we could simply float away to safety – or perhaps we should just need a balloon, since you yourself seem to providing all the hot-'

I held up a hand. 'You know my methods, Holmes!' I said with mock severity. 'Do you know the literary term "deus ex machina", at all?'

He stared at me. 'A trumpery device, much used by writers whose lack of imagination is outdone only by their lack of ability. Something entirely incredible which rescues the protagonist from an impossible situation in the nick of time.'

'Just so,' I said. 'Although your own solutions often seem to be reached by rather fanciful techniques.' And as he frowned, I went on hastily, 'But enough of this banter. We may not have sheets to tear up, but we do have something just as good.' And I removed my dustcoat to reveal the true nature of my 'padding,' a stout rope that lay coiled upon my chest and stomach.

Holmes clapped his hands softly. 'Well done, Doctor! I shall never doubt you again.'

I felt that was being overly optimistic, but accepted the praise as modestly as I could manage. 'I was always bothered by the thoughts of these high windows,' I told him. 'The trouble is, my rope is only a hundred feet long, so I don't think it will quite reach, especially as we must make one end secure, but it will get us out of this room, at any rate.'

'It will do splendidly,' said Holmes. 'I ought to have

thought of it myself. Just as well you were here, Watson.'

We secured the rope, passed it through the window, and studied its disposition. As I had said, it did not reach the ground, but its farther end lay well down the rock face. 'I think I could manage the rest,' said Holmes thoughtfully, and before I had realized what he intended, he had clambered through the open window and was shinning down the rope, hand over hand.

Von Gratz and I watched, scarcely daring to breathe, much less speak, as Holmes went down the rope. Where the castle wall began, he paused, there was evidently a rudimentary ledge, or at least a toe-hold of some sort, and Holmes stood there for a moment to get his bearings. Then he was off again, clinging on to the rope and finding what purchase he could for his feet in the solid rock. He did not descend the full length of the rope, but halted some ten feet above the far end. There was a ledge of sorts there, and he was able to release his grip on the rope and stand there, waving to indicate that we should follow.

'After you, Doctor,' said von Gratz.

I gritted my teeth, took a firm hold of the rope, and set off down towards Holmes.

I cannot say with any degree of honesty that I enjoyed the experience, or that I should care to repeat it. The first part was perhaps the worst, for the walls of the castle were relatively smooth, with only the occasional crack in the mortar between the great blocks of granite to aid the climber. Like Holmes, I paused for breath at the little ledge where the masonry met the sheer rock, then set off once more. Although the cliff looked massive and precipitous from a distance, it was not by any means as smooth as the castle wall had been, and I was able to find some footholds to assist my descent. In a fairly short while, and without much real difficulty – though not without some trepidation! – I had reached Holmes, and he stretched out a hand to help me find the tiny ledge upon which he stood. 'Well done, Watson!' And he waved to von Gratz to join us.

As I watched von Gratz climb down, and then held out a hand to him just as Holmes had done for me, Holmes was busy examining the cliff below us, and when von Gratz had arrived at our little ledge, now woefully overcrowded, Holmes told us, 'There is a path of sorts. Follow me,' and off he went.

I suppose that a very small and delicate mountain goat might have called it a 'path', and possibly those hardy souls who spend their summer holidays in the Alps might have strolled down it with ease, but frankly I think that the word invested it with a dignity it did not possess. It did provide a foothold of sorts, though, and pointed us the way we had to travel. And then Holmes always kept himself in peak condition, von Gratz was fresh from his army duties, and although I was probably the most out of condition, even I myself usually walked on my rounds, so that we were all physically fit, and so we managed pretty well, all told.

For a few paces we could almost walk upright, then came a short steep climb, another stretch of 'path', many a missed step, many a muffled curse, a few bad moments as loose shale or gravel gave way beneath our feet, and we came at last to a spot a few feet from the ground, from which we could jump or slide, according to our inclinations, to safety.

So down we came, dirty and dusty, all three of us bruised and grazed, and with the knees of our trousers in a state that would break the hearts of our various tailors, but free at last.

'Our primary task,' said Holmes, 'is to establish that Gottfried and Karl have indeed left the castle.'

Von Gratz nodded, and led us to the first house in the little village, where we soon found that Duke Gottfried and his entourage had indeed left the place early that same morning, taking the one and only road out of the place, that is, heading towards Marienburg. 'If only we had left earlier!' said von Gratz as he translated this from the local dialect for us. 'Or if we had not detoured to make those other deliveries. We might have encountered them on the road, and done something to forestall them.'

Holmes shook his head. 'In any event, unless we had spotted them within the town itself, our grocer's cart and old Dobbin there would scarcely have kept up with a carriage and pair. No, they have the advantage for the moment, and all we can do is follow them, and hope to use our wits to make up for the start they have on us. It is surely logical to suppose that they have taken the train to the capital, is it not? Unless, that is, Duke Gottfried has another bolt-hole somewhere in the countryside?'

'The castle and lands here are the only sort of country estate that I know of,' said von Gratz. 'Gottfried has a town house in Dopzhe, and I can only assume that he is headed there.'

We set off on foot, without troubling about the horse and cart; von Gratz said that if it were not recovered, he or the king would compensate old Tommaso Valentini. It was perhaps three miles as the crow flies to Marienburg, but the road wound in a fantastic fashion through the forests, making the true distance double what the map would suggest. But von Gratz recalled a few foresters' paths and short cuts, and we arrived at the outskirts of the town in a little over an hour and a half.

Our next task was to enquire at the railway station whether anyone had noticed Duke Gottfried taking a train. We were out of luck; though the ticket collector did tell us that several gentlemen who more or less resembled the duke's general appearance had taken trains that morning. And that was all the result of our journey to Schloss Württemburg! The possibility that Gottfried and Karl had remained in Marienburg was considered, and discounted, for there seemed no good reason why they should move from the safety of the castle to the comparative danger and discomfort of some hotel.

All we could do was follow them back to Dopzhe. There was a train in a little under an hour, just time for us to return to our modest lodgings, pay our bill and collect our bags, and that is what we did.

We had the compartment to ourselves, and Holmes sat in one corner, his face set, deep in thought and ignoring any remarks that von Gratz or I ventured to address to him. After half an hour, though, Holmes looked across at us and laughed in his odd silent fashion. 'Not one of our best efforts, Watson,' he said. 'If you write this up, you will have to make great play of the difficulties and dangers of our escape, to distract attention from our ignominious failure.'

'If I must.'

'And do not hesitate to mention, and perhaps even to exaggerate, your own magnificent part in our getaway.'

'I shall, never fear! But what is our next move, Holmes?'

'Well, Gottfried and Karl have clearly decided that the castle is no safe place.' Holmes frowned, shook his head. 'And yet one would surely be hard pressed to think of anywhere safer! It is a puzzle, is it not?'

'Their perceived danger is surely not to them, though,

but to the papers,' I said. 'Would those not be safe in the bank? Or with their lawyers?'

Holmes shook his head. 'Both very obvious places.'

'And they would not want the papers too far away,' von Gratz added.

'Then that leaves only Gottfried's town house, and surely that is more obvious yet?' I said. 'The very first place anyone would look.'

'Ah, but Gottfried might be playing a deep game, trusting to the fact that it is too obvious to bother with.'

'What, like the chap in Poe's story, "The Pilfered Letter" – no, "Purloined", that was it. That what you mean?'

'I think it must be our starting point,' said Holmes, and lapsed into a moody silence yet again.

He could be right, I reflected. If a man has a house, and wants to keep something safe and close at hand, then that house is an obvious place; but then if a man also has a castle, it surely makes more sense to remain there, with the gate secured! I could not for the life of me see why Gottfried had chosen to let us in; why, given that he knew we were coming, had he not simply shut us out? It made no sort of sense that I could see. And it certainly makes no sense to keep valuable papers at home if a man has bankers, lawyers, men with safes and strongrooms. It was all very well for Holmes to think that Gottfried would try to outsmart us; but if Gottfried thought that Holmes thought that he – Gottfried – thought – oh, damnation! I thought. I was never any good at this arguing in a circle, and I gave it up. Holmes, as I had thought at the outset, was right; for if we searched Gottfried's house and did not find the papers, then we could always try his bank or his lawyer next!

We returned to the Albion Hotel, and it speaks volumes for the management of the place that they did not turn us out, or even raise a questioning eyebrow at our dishevelled state; only the manager ventured in a low tone to recommend a laundress who had, he said, great skill in the art of invisible mending.

As we were making for the stairs, the manager called to me, 'Oh, Doctor Watson! There was a telegram for you.' And he handed me a little square buff envelope.

My first thought was naturally that something untoward had happened to Mary, and my heart sank. I should, I reflected as I tore the envelope open, never have left her in London with Mrs Norton; indeed, had I not thought as much at the outset, had I not asked Holmes for reassurance on the point, aye, and been given it? What was that reassurance worth now, pray? But then my eye lit on the signature, 'Mary,' and my spirits soared.

'From my wife,' I said.

'Indeed?' said Holmes.

'Yes – oh! That's odd.'

'Indeed?' said Holmes a second time.

'Indeed, Holmes. Listen to this: "Gone away. Take care, my – " ' – well, the rest is neither here nor there. But what on earth can Mary mean by "Gone away", I wonder?'

'Oh, I rather think that is intended for me,' said Holmes. 'Though I do not dispute your claim to the rest of it,' he added with a twinkle in his eye. 'You see, "Gone away" was the phrase I had agreed with Mrs Watson should be used in the event that Mrs Norton absconded from your house.'

'I see! Yes, I recall that you predicted something of the kind. The telegraph office stamp shows that Mary sent it yesterday, just after noon, so presumably Mrs Norton made good her escape yesterday morning. We might reasonably expect her tomorrow, then, or the day after?'

Holmes nodded. 'I fancy she will lose no time getting here.'

'But why? What object can she possibly have in coming here? Having sought our help, why does she not simply let us get on with it?'

'Ah, there you have me,' said Holmes. 'Unless, of course, she doubts our ability to solve the problem – and, on our recent showing, one cannot entirely blame her there!' He smiled, and added, 'But doubtless all will be made clear in due course.'

When once von Gratz had made himself a little more presentable in the hotel, he left us and went to the palace, returning towards evening with the news that Duke Gottfried was indeed in the capital, and had been invited to call upon the king on the following day.

'That is fortunate,' I said.

Von Gratz laughed. 'I myself suggested it to His Majesty, thinking it might be as well to get Gottfried out of his house for a time, so that we can make a preliminary reconnaissance. It will not be possible to enter the house in daylight, of course, more especially since Karl will still be inside – for he will not wish to show himself in public just yet. Still, we can study the exterior, I think.'

'It was well thought of,' said Holmes. 'We should be able to make out our prospective entrance, and make a return visit somewhat later tomorrow, when they are all asleep.'

'Holmes?' I asked.

'Yes?'

'You do not think that it might be another trap, do you? This house, so conveniently situated here in the town?

After all, if we break in then we are in the wrong, to the casual onlooker at any rate. Gottfried would be well within his rights to have his servants shoot us like dogs, and claim we were common burglars.'

'H'mm. It is an interesting thought. Von Gratz?'

'It is the sort of thing Gottfried might think of, it is true.' He stood up. 'Leave it with me. I shall see you this evening, for dinner,' and he saw himself out.

Holmes now proposed to smoke in silence for a while, and think the matter over. I preferred to rest, reflecting that we might be in for an exciting time on the morrow. Towards the dinner hour I bathed and changed, and then sought out Holmes, whom I found still smoking his old briar. 'We had engaged to see von Gratz,' I reminded him, and he smiled and stood up.

When Holmes was ready, we went downstairs. We had expected von Gratz to meet us in the hotel lobby, but instead he sent his coach, with a request that we go to his private apartments. A drive of some ten minutes brought us to the house, an old building discreetly tucked away in a leafy suburb.

Von Gratz had rooms on the first floor, and as we entered we saw that he had another visitor, a tall young man in the same uniform as that which von Gratz himself wore. 'Mr Holmes, Doctor Watson, this is Captain Markus, of my own regiment of hussars,' von Gratz told us.

Markus shook my hand. I liked his grip, firm but not belligerent, and I liked the look of him; though outwardly serious, there was yet a twinkle in his eye that showed he would be an excellent companion.

'Captain Markus will go with us tomorrow night,' said von Gratz. 'He will wait outside –' Markus made as if to object to this, but von Gratz waved him to silence – 'and in the event that we do not reappear in, shall we say, an hour, the captain will fetch some of his own men and effect an entry, to see what has become of us. Will that serve?'

'It will,' said Holmes. 'And I may say that I shall feel happier knowing that Captain Markus is waiting outside.'

I echoed this sentiment. Frankly I thought that the whole affair had the air of a trap, and I should be happier knowing that we had allies who were ready and willing to come to our aid. And as dinner progressed, and it became clear that Markus – in common with much of the army, I gathered – was no friend of Duke Gottfried, I formed the impression that von Gratz had given Markus another order which he had not mentioned to Holmes and myself; namely, that if Gottfried and Karl did us any harm, then Markus was to avenge us. As I say, it was but an impression; yet it was exactly what I should have done myself, and Markus did not seem the sort of man who would cavil at avenging a friend. So by the end of the meal, I was feeling considerably more cheerful than when I sat down at the table.

I mentioned something of this to Holmes as we were driven back to the Albion later that night. He nodded. 'It is certainly reassuring,' he said. 'It means that we can get on with our search without worrying too much about being detected.'

SIX

On the following morning, we rose bright and early. Von Gratz called upon us, and we walked to Gottfried's town house, situated in its own gardens in a broad boulevard, not unlike those which lead to the Bois in Paris – I believe I told you that the architect of Dopzhe had used the French capital as a model. There was a great high wall round the gardens, an iron gate, ten feet or so high, and a lodge, evidently occupied by a gate-keeper or watchman, just inside the gate. For good measure, there were gas lamps at either side of the gate.

Holmes shook his head, dissatisfied. 'Let us take a look at the back,' he said.

We walked to the end of the road, and turned down a quiet back street, little more than a mews, that ran behind the boulevard. Holmes went on, counting the houses carefully, until he slowed down near a low building, evidently the stables and coach house for Gottfried's mansion. The wall here was by no means as high as that at the front, and I noticed Holmes's smile of satisfaction. He strolled on, past the outbuildings and wooden gate, slowing down twenty feet beyond.

'There will be people in the stables,' I said, 'so we cannot use the gate.'

'True,' said Holmes, 'but I can undertake to climb the wall

here, and if we do so at the far end of the garden, we should be unobserved by anyone in the vicinity of the stables.'

'And what of access to the house?'

'Did you not remark the ivy, or some such creeper, round the back? If we cannot reach a window it will be a poor thing. And in any event there are the sort of French windows at the front of the house that any child could open.'

We returned to the hotel, and passed the remainder of the day somehow or other. Von Gratz had left us, saying that he needed to discuss plans with Captain Markus, so Holmes and I were left alone. I must say that we made a precious pair. Holmes was uncommunicative, and I too was disinclined for conversation, being somewhat concerned as to the prospects for success. To be blunt, the more I thought about this scheme, the less I liked it. Still, I could think of no alternative that might hold a better chance of working, so I had to make the best of it.

It was in no happy frame of mind that I saw the light fade that evening. Holmes bestirred himself, and remarked that it was nearly time to leave. When I ventured to mention dinner, Holmes waved a hand impatiently, and repeated his oft-made observation that he seldom ate whilst working. I had not had any great appetite myself, but in the paradoxical, contrary way of humanity, Holmes's remark made me disputatious, and I not only had an excellent dinner myself but actually prevailed upon Holmes to join me, though he only picked at the splendid fare before him. Still, he did eat a little, so I felt that I had made some progress.

We had promised to meet von Gratz outside the hotel at seven, and were there prompt to our time. Von Gratz, dressed in sober black and wrapped in a cloak, emerged from the shadows, Markus by his side. 'All is arranged,' von Gratz told us. 'Markus will keep watch, and his men will not be far away, so we have nothing to fear.'

The hour was, of course, rather early for burglary, at least if Gottfried and his guests were dining at home. But we had hopes that they might be dining out that evening, and if that proved to be the case then we should go in more or less as they went out. The servants, with no pressing duties, would not be very alert, and we ought to be able to work unsuspected and undetected. That was the theory, at any rate.

Our first task was thus to keep watch at the front of the house, to see if its inhabitants left. Should they fail to do so, then we must move our base of operations to the narrow lane at the back, and wait until all the lights went out, a task which promised to be long and dreary.

It looked, though, as if we were in luck, for just after half past seven, there was some activity at the front gate. A carriage came rattling round the corner from the direction of the mews, and pulled up by the gate. Two men strolled down the drive from the house, and halted by the carriage whilst one of them lit a cigar. We were just across the road, in our own carriage, and the two men stood almost directly beneath a street lamp, so we had no difficulty seeing them.

Both men were tall, slender. The man lighting the cigar was a good deal muffled up, his opera hat pulled down, a scarf round the lower part of his face, and the collar of his cloak turned well up. Obviously he had to shift this drapery somewhat in order to accomplish the task of getting his cigar burning properly, but then he turned his head away from us as he applied vesta to corona, so that we still could not get a proper look at his face. The other man was bare-headed, his hat in his hand, and he seemed to stare directly at us, so that instinctively I settled lower in the seat of the carriage. This second man had an unworldly look about him, almost a monastic asceticism, that seemed oddly at ease with his costume of man about town.

Von Gratz nudged me in the ribs. 'That is Gottfried,' he said. 'Looks like a clergyman, does he not? I do not know the other fellow, the one wrapped up like a mummy.'

'I take it that is Karl?' said Holmes.

'You are probably right,' said von Gratz.

'Highly convenient,' I said. 'In fact they could not have fallen in better with our plans had they joined in our discussions!'

'H'mm,' said Holmes.

'And what does that mean?'

'As you say, Watson, it is highly convenient. Of course, it would have been even more convenient for Gottfried and his guest had the coachman taken the carriage up the drive from the stables to the front door, instead of coming all the long way round to the gate, thereby obliging Gottfried and the other fellow to walk from the house.'

'You mean they want us to see them leaving? You suspect a trap, then?'

'Say rather that I suspect they are playing a deep game.'

I sank back in my seat. A trap? If not, then why should Gottfried advertise his absence? It almost seemed as if he wanted us to search the place! And why on earth should he want that, unless – 'Unless,' I said out loud, 'they have the papers on them?'

Holmes stared at me.

'Never,' said von Gratz. 'It would be far too dangerous

for them to consider it. They know that there is always the possibility of being waylaid and searched.' He looked at Markus, sitting opposite. 'On the other hand, Gottfried may indeed play a deep game. By Heaven, if I thought that they *did* have the papers on them –!'

Holmes raised a hand. 'As you say, they will have made due allowance for all that. Our own plans are made, so let us by all means stick to them. With Captain Markus and his men outside, we have little to fear, whatever arrangements Gottfried may have made to welcome us.'

'And I have my pistol, this time,' I told him, patting my pocket. 'I have no intention of being imprisoned a third time!'

Von Gratz laughed, and patted his own pocket in imitation of my action. 'I too am armed,' he said. 'The only danger I foresee is that Karl may have sent another man with Gottfried, to fool us, while Karl himself remains in the house. But we are three to one, even in that event. And I may add that if I do find Karl in there, and he becomes troublesome, I shall shoot him like a dog. Oh, I beg your pardon, I had forgotten you were English – like a rat, then, if you will.' And he gave a laugh that boded ill for Karl in the event that he were in the house.

Holmes looked at him sternly. 'It is less a matter of revenge than of helping the king.' At which von Gratz tried unconvincingly to look abashed, though I was certain that he had made up his mind to kill Karl, should the occasion arise.

Gottfried and his companion got into their carriage, and rattled off at a good pace. Holmes glanced at his watch. 'We shall give them ten minutes,' he decided, 'by which time the servants should have settled down to their own suppers. And then we three shall visit the back wall, and you, Captain Markus, will remain here. I think if you will allow us one hour and a half, by which time we should be back to report success, and if not –'

'If not, sir, I know what to do,' said Markus, touching the butt of his revolver in a significant fashion.

We waited our ten minutes, perhaps not quite the longest ten minutes I ever spent, but long enough for me. And then Holmes led the way to the little mews at the back of the house, and we took a closer look at the wall. There was a broad enough gate for the coach and so on, with a little postern door affair in it, but we dared not try these. Instead we got as far away from the gate and outbuildings as we could, and shinned over the wall, which at that point was only some six or seven feet high – a mere nothing compared to our descent from the castle such a short time before!

The garden at the spot where we entered was grown up with rhododendrons or some such shrubs, ideal cover for miscreants such as ourselves. Holmes cautiously parted the leaves and peered out, then motioned to us to follow him across the manicured lawn. We had not been able to see this part of the house properly from the lane, but we now made out a fairly elaborate French window, evidently designed to give the owners of the house easy access to the gardens in the fine weather. However, these windows were locked on the inside, and Holmes took one look at them and shook his head. I moved a few paces to one side and examined a little door set in a neat porch, but that too was securely fastened, and I began to think that it would be an undignified scramble up the ivy which grew thick over part of the wall. But the slightest of sounds from Holmes showed me that he had opened a side window.

We climbed inside, and could just make out that we were in some sort of reception room, spacious enough to hold a regiment of dancers. My heart sank within me, and I muttered in Holmes's ear, 'How on earth can we search the entire house, much less do it in an hour?'

I sensed, rather than saw, his impatient shake of the head. 'The papers cannot be in any public room, that would be far too dangerous. They must be in Gottfried's private apartments, or in Karl's. We shall make our way upstairs,' and off he went towards the door.

I have said that the room into which we had broken was in darkness; but the servants were still in the house, and their master was expected back later that same evening, so the entrance hall and corridors were still lighted by gas lamps. Indeed, the whole ground floor was a sight too well lit for my taste. But Holmes never showed any hesitation, moving swiftly and silently to the great staircase, and darting up the stairs without a sound.

The first floor was not quite so brightly lit as the ground floor, with only an occasional gas-jet, turned down low, casting a pool of light in the corridor here and there. Holmes had brought along a dark lantern for each of us, and we now lit these. 'We shall work faster if we split up,' Holmes told us in a whisper, and he waved his hand to indicate the direction in which von Gratz and I were to go, before opening the nearest door and vanishing inside.

I tried a couple of rooms, clearly guest bedrooms, and unoccupied, before opening the door of a room that was somewhat grander than the others, and which had obvious signs of being used; a night-shirt laid out on the bed, slippers ready to hand – or foot – and the like. I waved to Holmes and von Gratz to join me.

Von Gratz picked up a silver hair brush and looked at the crest engraved upon it. 'It is Gottfried's coat of arms,' he said.

Holmes threw the beam of his lantern round the room, stopping it as it illuminated a connecting door to the next room. 'A sitting room?' He opened the door, and we saw that it was indeed a compound of sitting room and study, being furnished with comfortable chairs, but having book-shelves on the whole of one wall.

This looked more like it, I reflected, as I followed Holmes into the room. We should be unlucky indeed if we did not find what we sought here. Then my train of thought was broken, and I let out a muffled curse as my ankle struck some solid object on the floor.

The impact had made a slight thud, and Holmes made a sound, 'Shh!' of disapproval. Irked at myself for my careless-ness, I cast the beam of my own lantern down, to see what I had bumped into. It was a little revolving bookcase made of oak, a couple of feet high, just the right height for a man to reach from the depths of the leather armchair which stood nearby. A dainty looking thing, but solidly built, as my ankle could testify! I had seen something like it in London the previous year, and thought that I would like one for my own little den, and now I wished I had bought it.

Then I looked again. There were books on the little shelves, but there were also illustrated magazines. Now, earlier on I had mentioned something about Poe's 'Pur-loined Letter,' and this little bookcase reminded me irresistibly of that story; for if I wanted a safe place to hide letters, I should interleave them into a book or an illustrated weekly paper, and put the whole thing out in public view. I bent down, and took some of the magazines from their shelves, riffling the pages in the hope that some loose sheets would flutter down. Nothing. Disappointed, I tried again. And again, nothing. Only – as I flicked the pages over, something seemed odd about them. I held my lantern nearer, and examined the magazine more carefully. Yes! Here and there, a letter had been inserted, fixed by gumming one long edge to the spine of the magazine so that the sheets did not fall out when the thing was held upside down and shaken. I called Holmes to see.

'Well, done!' he said. 'It is a clever device, and one which a clever man might have missed.' – Which I took to be a compliment! He showed the letters to von Gratz. 'Is it the king's handwriting? His seal?'

Von Gratz studied the letters closely. 'It appears to be the king's hand,' he said cautiously. 'If it is not, it is an excellent forgery.'

'But then it would be, would it not? It would have to be,' said Holmes, his tone far removed from the initial elation of a moment before. 'Is the photograph there?' he asked me.

I rummaged again amongst the books and so forth on the stand. 'There is a photograph album here,' I said. 'Working on the premise that the obvious thing is the correct thing –' and I took the squat, heavy, leather-bound album from its shelf and began to turn the pages. Most of the pictures were the size which the photographers call 'cabinet', some four inches by five, mounted on heavy card, and with tissue paper to protect them. They were of the usual sort, family portraits of absorbing interest to those depicted in them, mildly amusing to those family members not so portrayed, and stultifyingly boring to the outsider. But among the family groups, the old dowager duchesses, the young boys in sailor suits, was one picture which made us all three gasp aloud as I turned the page. It was the duplicate of that which Mrs Norton had shown us, the very photograph which all the fuss was about!

'But this is merely a print,' von Gratz reminded us. 'We must still find the original plate.' And he stood up, as if to search elsewhere.

I was still sure that I alone had solved the case, though, and I continued to turn the pages of my little album. As I did so, it seemed that one page was thicker and heavier than the rest, and I studied it more closely. The photograph in the mount was of an elderly lady in the stiff pose and formal dress of perhaps 1860; but when I lifted a corner of this photograph, I found a glass plate beneath it. As I have said, the photographs were mounted on stout card, and two pages of this card had been cemented together, with the centre of the uppermost cut out to form a recess.

I held the thing aloft in triumph.

'Is that authentic?' asked Holmes.

Von Gratz took the plate from me, and shone his light on it. 'It is difficult to be sure,' he said. 'It is what we call a "negative", and without making a print from it, I cannot swear as to details.'

I could see his difficulty. The beam of the lantern reflected from the silver surface, making it hard to distinguish anything, at least for my untutored gaze. The photograph showed a man and a woman, that was clear, and the costumes seemed in general not unlike those in the print; but the tones were all reversed, so that the woman's hair was white, and her face a dark grey.

Von Gratz shook his head. 'It appears to be my plate,' he said, but there was doubt in his voice.

'It is too pat,' said Holmes, and his voice was decisive. 'I know that it is –' and he stopped, as von Gratz gave a sharp intake of breath. 'Well?'

'It is a forgery!' said von Gratz. 'That is, the plate is genuine enough, but this is not the picture which I took.'

'You are certain?'

'Absolutely. You see, I am a keen photographer, and I like to experiment with new chemicals, new techniques. It is not an exact science, you understand, the nature of the plate has its effect, the chemicals, the temperature of the developing solution –'

'Yes, yes!' said Holmes, with a good deal of impatience.

'To be brief, a small section of my plate was spoiled, the gelatine was overheated and crinkled, "reticulated", as we call it. It was no great matter in the print, in fact it looks merely like a small fleecy cloud. But I am an amateur in the true sense, Mr Holmes, and it rankled with me. This plate, though, is perfect, with no defects in the gelatine at all.'

'A fake?' I said. 'It is an elaborate charade, though! They have hired a photographer, an actor and actress –'

'Elaborate, yes,' said Holmes. 'But worthwhile if it chanced to throw us off the scent. I knew it was too good to be true!' He thought a brief moment, then laughed and took up one of the magazines which contained the letters. 'We must work fast,' he said, 'for we still have to find the real papers. But we can use the fakes, none the less.' And he started to run the blade of his penknife down the spine of the magazine to free the letters.

'You plan to switch them?' I asked.

'Oh, an obvious enough jest, but I cannot resist it. There were twenty-three, were there not, according to Mrs Norton?'

'Ah – that was the number I recall,' I said, perfectly untruthfully.

'Then all are present.'

'But, Holmes, you yourself said we do not have the real letters and photograph! Where are they?'

'The logical place is a safe. And the safe is –' and Holmes darted about, moving pictures on the walls, tapping the books on the shelves, until he laughed, and finished – 'And the safe is here!' as a section of 'books', actually merely painted wood, slid aside to reveal a smart modern safe.

'Small, but effective,' Holmes remarked, as he studied the dial. 'The new type, you see, where the owner chooses some word of his own to act as the key. H'mm, five letters, "A" to "Z". How many possible combinations is that, I wonder?'

'Too many! Wait, though – if the safe is new, may it not have been bought specifically for this one task? If so, then the word is –'

'"Adler"! To be sure.' Holmes spun the little dials, and tried the handle. It did not budge.

'H'mm. If my mathematics are not too rusty, the number is twenty-six to the power five. A number near enough astronomical.'

'Not to speak of all those umlauts,' I added helpfully. 'It is a German safe.'

'Nay, it is made by Hyder and Levin, an American firm, so that lessens our task,' said Holmes with a laugh. Then he snapped his fingers. 'We are too formal, Doctor. We should perhaps adopt the American usage for the American safe,' and he spun the dials again until the wheel read 'Irene', and tried the handle a second time.

With the softest of clicks the handle turned, and the door swung open. Holmes gave a quiet laugh of triumph as he took from the safe a leather document case. He opened the case, and removed the contents. 'I fancy these are the genuine papers,' said he, handing a glass plate to von Gratz.

Von Gratz scrutinized the plate. 'It is the real plate,' he said. 'There is the little patch of reticulated gelatine.'

'Capital! Then we put the real papers to one side, and the fakes go into the case, and the case into the safe,' said Holmes, suiting his actions to the words. The fakes which I had discovered in the bookcase were quickly lodged in the safe, and the safe locked.

'They will surely detect the imposition?' I said.

'Oh, to be sure. But it will not be immediately, at least I hope not. And in any event, it will be too late. I just hope Gottfried and Karl appreciate the joke, though I rather fear they will not.' Holmes looked at his watch. 'We are almost over-staying our welcome, and Captain Markus will be anxious.' He cast the beam of his lantern round the room. 'I think that all is in order. We may have disarranged one or two pieces of furniture, but that is quite consistent with our removal of the "fake" papers. Come, gentlemen, it is time we were off.'

We returned to Markus, who was indeed beginning to get a touch restive, and the four of us returned to the Albion. As we sat in the carriage a sort of nervous reaction set in with me, for it had all seemed so easy that I feared some twist in the tail of our little adventure. And I fancy that the others felt the same way, for none of us seemed inclined to say a word. But the return was quite uneventful, and we were soon safe in our rooms. Not until then did we venture to relax somewhat, and Holmes poured us all a stiff drink.

'I wonder what the best thing to do with it might be?' said Holmes, referring to the glass plate which he was holding up to the light.

'Smash the damned thing in a million pieces!' suggested von Gratz. 'That way, it can harm no-one ever again.'

'It is an interesting proposition,' said Holmes.

'But, Holmes!' I said.

'Yes, Watson?'

'Mrs – that is, your client –'

'Ah, yes, I had all but forgotten,' said Holmes. He smiled at von Gratz. 'My client, as Watson does well to remind me, is Mrs Norton, and it is to her that the photograph should rightly be returned.'

'But it was I who took the photograph,' von Gratz told him. 'Have I no say in its disposition, then?'

'Forgive me, but did you not give the photograph to Mrs Norton, or Miss Adler as she then was?'

'Why –' von Gratz hesitated – 'yes, it is true, but then it seemed so harmless, the act of one friend to another. I never envisaged that it would be used in this dreadful fashion. Surely that alters matters quite considerably? My first duty is to the king, and not to Mrs Norton.'

Holmes frowned, deep in thought. 'It is a good point,' he conceded at length. 'However, there are reasons why I should not destroy the plate just yet.'

'And what reasons are those?' asked von Gratz, naturally enough.

'I would prefer to keep them to myself for the moment.'

I could see that neither von Gratz nor Markus liked the sound of this; but equally I knew that Holmes must be thinking of the curious way in which the case had been brought to his attention, and the way Mrs Norton had insisted on the plate's being returned to her. Not that Holmes was necessarily going to return the plate to Mrs Norton, of course! But his inherent curiosity would prompt him to keep the plate until he knew the whole truth. And besides, as I – not to speak of the long-suffering Mrs Hudson, his landlady – knew only too well, Holmes had a constitutional aversion to throwing anything away, or destroying anything.

Holmes was saying, 'I think I shall keep the plate here, for the time being. You may rely upon me to find a safe place of concealment.'

Von Gratz and Markus took the liberty of disagreeing with this proposition, and some lively discussion ensued. It was all in good humour, though, for we all four believed that the hardest part of our task was done. After all, we had the papers, and could now dispose of them as we saw fit; and that was the important thing.

At about this time, I left the room – we were in the sitting room which Holmes and I shared jointly – for a few moments, on some trifling personal errand, I think to wash my hands or perhaps to fetch a pipe from my bedroom. I made my way back, but paused with my hand on the door. Something was different – I did not actually define it as 'wrong' at that moment, you are to understand, but there was that which made me hesitate, and attempt to work out what was changed. I have said that we were a merry party; and I think you would agree that, given our successful enterprise that evening, given that we had saved the king from disgrace, and Bohemia from civil war, we had every right to be merry.

And yet now the room was silent. No clink of glasses, no boisterous chaff, no sound of any voice. Wait, though! A woman's voice; more, one that I recognized as Mrs Norton's. So, Holmes was right; Mrs Norton had returned, to claim her precious 'papers', then.

I threw the door open, stepped inside, then stopped dead in my tracks. Mrs Norton was indeed there. She was saying something like, 'You must hand it over, Mr Holmes.'

I say, 'something like.' I cannot swear as to her exact words, for what caught my immediate attention, putting all other thoughts out of my mind for the moment, was that Holmes, von Gratz and Markus were all standing at one side of the room; while Mrs Norton, on the other side of the room, was pointing a small revolver at them.

SEVEN

When I opened the door, of course, I had not the remotest idea that Mrs Norton was threatening my companions with a pistol. I thus had no thoughts of concealment, I saw no need to enter quietly, or anything of the sort. I simply pushed the door open and walked into the room.

I have said that I noticed the little tableau; Holmes and the others at one side, Mrs Norton at the other. As I entered the room, they all turned to look at me, and for the briefest of moments we all simply stood there.

Then Holmes leaped at Mrs Norton, with von Gratz and Markus hard upon his heels. There was a somewhat undignified, and I must say a very gentlemanly, scramble, and before I had time to work out what exactly was going on, Holmes was holding the revolver, von Gratz and Markus were standing there looking about as bemused as I felt, while Mrs Norton was holding a handkerchief to her eyes and sobbing.

'My dear lady,' I said. 'What on earth is the meaning of all this?'

And the others echoed this sentiment, in more or less robust terms. For a considerable time Mrs Norton could not bring herself to speak, and then she told us, 'You have spoiled everything! My life is ruined!'

This was, I felt, a touch harsh. We had, after all, done

what Mrs Norton herself had asked of us, namely, saved the king from an apparently hopeless situation. What had we done wrong, then? Why this complaint, and above all why the revolver? I was completely lost, and rather offended, by Mrs Norton's behaviour, and I fancy that the others felt much the same. Von Gratz frowned, Markus put a hand to his head, while Holmes looked thoughtful.

'It is essential that I have the photograph back,' Mrs Norton said, her composure much recovered.

'But Irene – madame – you need have no fears. The photograph is quite safe with us,' said von Gratz. 'Our loyalty is to the king, after all.'

'As is mine. But then a wife has other loyalties, more pressing yet.'

'And what could be more important?' asked von Gratz.

'Why, a wife's loyalty to her husband,' answered Mrs Norton. 'In my case, to the best husband a woman ever had, my own dear Godfrey.'

'And what has Mr Norton to do with the matter?' asked Holmes quickly.

The answer was unexpected; Mrs Norton burst into tears a second time. Holmes looked at von Gratz and Markus. 'Gentlemen,' said he, 'it might be as well if you were to wait in the next room. I shall call you when we have resolved this little problem.'

As you may imagine, neither von Gratz nor Markus received this suggestion with any marked enthusiasm. But it was clear that Mrs Norton was not going to speak more coherently in what must have seemed a roomful of folk, and they went out, grumbling to themselves as they did so.

'And now, Mrs Norton,' said Holmes, as the door closed behind the others, 'you may speak freely. You are, after all, my original client, and my duty is to you, provided always that it does not conflict with my loyalty to the king.'

And, 'What's all this about your husband?' I asked.

Mrs Norton looked from one to the other of us. 'They have abducted Godfrey,' she said.

'What?' said Holmes.

'You mean Gottfried and Karl?' I asked. 'But why –'

'No, no! Gottfried and Karl have not taken him.'

'Who, then?'

Mrs Norton shook her head quickly. 'That, I cannot say for sure.'

'I think you had better start at the beginning,' said Holmes.

'You are right,' said Mrs Norton. 'Well, then, it was as I told you in London, in part at least. The papers were indeed stolen, just as I said, though I did not tell you the real circumstances.' She put a hand to her head, and I poured some water for her. 'Thank you, Doctor Watson. The first part of my account, the meeting with Karl, his persuading me to send the photograph to the King of Scandinavia, that was true, as was the part about meeting Godfrey, our deciding to leave London and live quietly, and so forth. But then I lied to you when I said there was an attempt at burglary; or at any rate, I should have said that the attempt succeeded. Yes, the papers were stolen, though I did not immediately realize that Karl was the thief, despite the fact that it was he who had persuaded me to threaten the king earlier. I thought earnestly about what I should do, and decided to send a warning to the king, to tell him I no longer had the papers. But then before I had done so, on the following morning, a strange man called at the house –'

'How "strange"?' asked Holmes.

'I mean partly that I did not know him; but partly that he looked – odd. I suspect he was wearing a wig, a disguise; as you are aware, Mr Holmes, I am no stranger to disguise myself, and I could swear that he was attempting to hide his real identity. Well, he represented himself to me as a detective. He said that there had been reports of burglaries, suspicious characters, in the neighbourhood, and he asked if I had seen or heard anything out of the ordinary, or if there had been any attempt to break into the house. Naturally, that increased my initial distrust of him, for none of the neighbours had ever mentioned anything of the sort to me. I at once associated him in my mind with the theft of the papers; but he made no threat, did not ask for money, or anything of that kind, as one might have expected. So what could I do? I merely told him that I would keep a look out, and he left.'

'And then?'

'Then, the next day again, that is, two days after the theft of the papers, I had been out, trying to think what to do. I had not sent a message to the king, as I had at first intended –'

'And why not?' asked Holmes.

Mrs Norton hesitated. 'To be frank, Mr Holmes, I half suspected that the suspicious man who had called upon me the previous day might be an agent of the king's. I have said that I did not know what to think, much less what to do. There seemed no-one to whom I could turn; indeed, I had not even told Godfrey about the theft of the papers, not wishing to stir up old and painful memories.' She hesitated again. 'I walked in the parks and the streets, my mind a whirl. I determined that at least I should tell Godfrey of the theft, ask his advice. I returned home, then, for Godfrey was at home, or so I thought. But when I arrived, I found that our private apartments had been ransacked, and Godfrey had vanished. I questioned the servants, and discovered that two men had called upon Godfrey earlier; neither they, nor Godfrey, had been seen to leave. I decided that enough was enough, and that I should call the police. I did not intend to mention the papers, of course, but merely to report Godfrey's abduction. But as I was about to send to the prefecture, a note was delivered – "You will be contacted", it read, "but do not call the police, as you value your husband's life". That was clear enough; I did as I was asked, and waited, though it was the longest wait I have ever known.

'A second message summoned me to a nearby café, and that odd man was there again. He ignored my pleas and protests; his first questions were about the papers, where were they, and so on. I told him they were stolen, and it was obvious that he did not believe me. I burst into tears, swore by all that I held sacred that it was true, swore by Godfrey's very life, and in the end I persuaded him to believe me. It was he who muttered, "That devil Karl", and thus identified the culprit. I saw at once that it was so, and – desperate to get Godfrey back – told him of the earlier episode with Karl. He seemed to believe me, and I had hopes that, now that there was no possibility of my handing the papers over, Godfrey would be freed. But then the dreadful man told me that it did not matter that Karl had the papers – if I wanted to see Godfrey alive, I must recover them! I cried, I protested, but to no avail. I then saw that I must do as he asked, and persuaded him to help me.'

'He took part in the charade in London, then, impersonating Karl?'

Mrs Norton nodded. 'I am truly sorry, Mr Holmes. But what else could I do? I thought that if I could get you to recover the papers from Karl and Gottfried, I could save Godfrey.'

I asked, 'But then, was the whole business about your being tied up a fake? I could have sworn you were in some distress.'

Mrs Norton managed a faint smile. 'My distress was real enough, Doctor, and for obvious reasons. For the rest, we could not tell if – or, rather, when – Mr Holmes would take our bait. My – "confederate", as I suppose I must call him, for I still have no notion of his real identity, untied me every so often, and I took a little water, and attended to my other needs. But we had to keep up the pretence.'

'This fellow was in the house, then, when we arrived?' asked Holmes quickly.

'That, I cannot say. I think not, for he crept in by the back door at intervals. It now occurs to me that he probably had a confederate of his own, to keep watch,' said Mrs Norton. 'That would be perfectly sensible, would it not? But it is merely surmise upon my part, for I knew nothing of what he was up to, apart from what I have told you.'

'H'mm. Well, madam, you would perhaps have done better to tell us this at the outset,' said Holmes. 'I wonder – if it is not Gottfried and Karl, then who has abducted Mr Norton?'

'The anarchists, perhaps?' I suggested.

'Oh, the anarchists, to be sure.' But there was an odd note in Holmes's voice.

'Well then, who else?' I asked him.

'I had thought, perhaps the king, as Mrs Norton suspected?'

'Doesn't make any sense, Holmes. The king has consulted you before, why should he not do so again, without any need for this rigmarole?'

'It is an interesting problem, is it not? Quite like one of your thrillers, Watson.'

'H'mm. A problem for any writer, though, Holmes. If the hero didn't do it, and the villains didn't do it, then who the devil *did* do it?' I recollected myself, and added hastily, 'I beg your pardon, Mrs Norton. I did not intend to make light of what must be a very distressing matter, but it is a pretty puzzle, I must say. Any ideas, Holmes?'

Holmes shrugged, and looked again at Mrs Norton. 'It is hardly the most pressing matter to demand our attention. Assuming that you had persuaded us to hand the papers back to you, what were you instructed to do then?'

'To place an advertisement in the "Personal" columns of the newspapers. I have a note of the wording here, some nonsense about "Irene wishes to inform her Papa that all is well now". I did not choose the code myself.'

'Indeed not.'

'Then "Papa" would reply in the same fashion, a newspaper advertisement telling me where to go to meet him.'

'And these advertisements were to be in the local papers? That is to say, the Bohemian papers?'

'Just so. The *Journal de Bohème*, the *Dopzhe Matin*, and so on.'

Holmes looked at me. 'Interesting.'

'As meaning that the villains – whoever they may be – are here in Bohemia? More, I would say that they were here in Dopzhe itself, for they could not rely upon the newspapers reaching an isolated rural spot in good time.'

'I agree,' said Holmes. 'Very well, suppose we place the

advertisement, and Watson and I go along to see who turns up? We might follow them, and I guarantee they would never see us.'

Mrs Norton shook her head. 'But they would know that I had betrayed them, and what price Godfrey's life then? Nobody else was supposed to know the form of the advertisement, so whether I go or not, they will know I have deceived them.'

Besides,' I pointed out, 'the appointed rendezvous will most likely be a café, or other public place. Some spot where the villains can observe Mrs Norton, check that she is not followed, before they make contact.'

'Doctor Watson is right,' said Mrs Norton. 'The only thing that will serve is for me to take the papers. I must, if I am to save Godfrey.'

'Impossible,' said Holmes with a quick shake of the head. 'Too dangerous by far. I must consider the king —'

'My husband's life is in your hands. You guaranteed to follow anyone who contacted me, did you not?'

'No, I merely guaranteed that they would not see me,' said Holmes, a touch nettled. 'However competent an investigator may be, there is always a risk that the quarry may elude him. Under any other circumstances I would risk it, but not as things are.'

'Then you are sentencing my husband to death.'

Holmes lifted a hand in genuine horror. 'You are asking me to choose between your husband's life, and the future of an entire country.'

'Yet you must choose,' said Mrs Norton calmly.

I put in, 'Holmes, there must be a way. I never yet knew you lose someone you were following, and —'

'It has happened,' he said.

'But – I shall be there, Holmes. And von Gratz, and Markus –'

He held up a hand to silence me. 'I know all that, Watson. But it is simply too risky. Why, before now I have accumulated evidence, set traps, had all the resources of Scotland Yard at my disposal – and still lost my man. You know it to be true, Doctor.'

I nodded, bitterly disappointed. 'It is so,' I told Mrs Norton. 'The possible risks to the king –'

'And the certain risk to Godfrey?'

Holmes said, 'We are perhaps looking at this from the wrong viewpoint, seeing one large problem where in reality there are two quite separate issues. One, the photograph, we have solved. The other, the matter of Mr Norton's abduction, we have still to consider. Tell me, madam, was any time limit set upon your recovering the papers?'

'Well, obviously I must recover them before the King of Scandinavia arrives. But apart from that, no, for I could hardly forecast how soon – if at all – you yourself would get the papers from Gottfried and Karl.'

'The mystery man won't know, Holmes,' I put in eagerly. 'Even Gottfried and Karl will – with a bit of luck – think we have only the forgeries.'

'Forgeries?' asked Mrs Norton.

Holmes waved a hand impatiently. 'A long story, madam. Yes, we may have a few days, perhaps even as long as a week, before they get restless. Mrs Norton, will you place your trust in Watson and myself?'

Mrs Norton thought for a moment. Then, 'I have no choice,' she said. 'But what if they become impatient and contact me, without waiting for me to place the advertisement?'

'In that case, you will simply tell them that you have approached me, asking for the return of the papers, but that I replied that I do not yet have them. Remember that they may not know whether that is true; and if somehow they know that I have the papers, and say as much, then you are to say that I must have lied to you, a perfectly logical proceeding under the circumstances. Accuse me of intransigence, of any vice in the calendar, but you must convince them that you have tried to get me to return the papers to you, and that I refused. Say that they must give you more time to persuade me. Do you understand?'

'Perfectly, Mr Holmes. And in turn I would ask you to remember that Godfrey's life is in your hands.'

'You may depend upon me, madam.' Holmes looked at me. 'Perhaps, Watson, you would be so good as to call in our friends?'

I did as he asked, and von Gratz and Captain Markus, both of them looking very puzzled, came back into the room. In a very few words Holmes told them what Mrs Norton had just told us.

Markus, honest and straightforward young fellow that he was, looked horrified as he heard of the unfortunate Godfrey Norton's abduction, and his hand went to the hilt of his sword, or at least to where his sword should have been.

Von Gratz, too, listened intently to Holmes's account, but there was a peculiar expression on his face, and when Holmes had finished, von Gratz asked quickly, 'And the photograph?'

'Ah, yes, the photograph. As I had hinted, I shall keep that myself, just for the time being. It will be safer that way.'

'Keep it,' said von Gratz, 'with a view to its possible use

in an exchange, an exchange for Mr Godfrey Norton, that is to say?'

'It is a remote possibility that we shall need it for that,' said Holmes, 'but still it is a possibility, and one that we must consider. After all, a man's life –'

'Is of no consequence,' said von Gratz, stepping forward and picking up the little revolver which Mrs Norton had so recently used to threaten him and the others. 'No, stay where you are, Mr Holmes, or I shall surely shoot you.'

'You traitorous dog!' I said.

Von Gratz laughed aloud.

'It was you who abducted Mr Norton!' I shouted.

Von Gratz laughed again, but then shook his head. 'I assure you, Doctor, that this unfortunate abduction is as distressing to me as it is to you. And it is as great a puzzle. But really, to call me a traitor, of all men! I promise you, no man deserves the name less than I, for – alone of those in this room – I have the king's interests at heart.'

'I say!' Markus protested, and I dare say that I too made some ineffectual remark.

Von Gratz waved these interruptions aside. 'So long as ever this plate remains intact,' he said, 'the king is in danger.' And before we could properly realize what he intended, he had raised the revolver and brought its butt down fair and square on the glass plate, which lay on a little table, shattering it into a thousand fragments.

'You fool!' cried Holmes.

And Mrs Norton said, 'Bertie – Baron von Gratz – I once called you friend, and believed you to be such. But now I must ask you never to speak to me again, for you have murdered my husband.' And with a dignity that was truly regal, she turned on her heel and walked from the room.

EIGHT

'I am sorry,' said von Gratz. 'But my first duty is to the king, and since the plate could still be used against him, it was part of that duty to destroy it.'

Holmes shook his head. 'You are right of course,' he said. 'And I am sorry that I called you a fool. But I had hopes that we could save both these unfortunate men, and now of course we cannot hope to use the plate to save Mr Norton.'

'Then we'll just have to use something else,' I said. 'Like our wits, for example. You yourself said that we might have as long as a week before anyone gets suspicious.'

Holmes smiled. 'You are right,' he said. 'Though I confess that I have not the slightest notion as to where we might start.' He looked a question at von Gratz.

'I have as little inspiration as you, Mr Holmes,' said von Gratz. 'Unless it is indeed these devils of anarchists who have abducted Mr Norton in an attempt to acquire the papers and thus bring down the king?'

'And do you have no clue as to the identity of these anarchists, no idea as to their meeting places?'

'The Ministry of Justice has, I believe, a department concerned with such matters,' said von Gratz. 'His Majesty will doubtless give me the authority to contact them, see what they know.'

'I confess that I cannot see that it will help us,' said

Holmes, 'but it is a start. More, it is the only starting place we have, so if you could make some discreet enquiries, and as soon as may be, I shall be grateful.'

'Tomorrow, I promise.'

'And can you think of no-one else who might be involved?' asked Holmes.

Von Gratz shook his head. 'Markus?'

Captain Markus said, 'I can think of nobody, sir. If it is not Gottfried – well! Who else would have any motive for such a cowardly proceeding?'

Holmes said, 'If it is not political, might it be more prosaic?' And when we looked blank, he went on, 'Might those who abducted Mr Norton have done so for money? Not to extort cash from Mrs Norton, but from the king?'

'Blackmail, you mean?' I asked.

'It would make sense, would it not?' said Holmes. 'If no-one with a claim to the throne has abducted the fellow, what is left? The king once told me that he would give an entire province of Bohemia to get the photograph back, so perhaps our unknown villains are looking to gain the cash equivalent of a province?'

Von Gratz nodded. 'It makes good sense. The king has much to lose, it would be worth a considerable sum to ensure that the treaty is signed without any inconvenience. Moreover, payment would be relatively safe, in that when once the treaty is signed, the photograph ceases to be a threat; there is thus no possibility of the criminals continually demanding payments in the future. The king would pay any amount, I am sure, especially if it were more or less a "once and for all" payment. I believe you are right, Mr Holmes.'

'Although that hardly gets us any further,' I muttered.

Holmes laughed. 'I would not say that, Watson. At least it shows us the direction in which we must look. And,' he added thoughtfully, 'it may point to the true culprit.'

Remember if you will that this was in 1889; it took only a moment for me to realize what Holmes meant. 'You mean – Professor Mor –'

He stopped me with a look. 'It makes sense, Watson.'

Von Gratz and Markus stared at us. Markus asked, 'You mean you know the identity of the criminal, Mr Holmes?'

'Say rather that I have my suspicions. Only time will tell if they are correct.'

With that, von Gratz and Markus had to be content. Von Gratz repeated his promise to contact the Ministry of Justice, to determine if possible whether their secret police had anything to tell us about the anarchists, and then he and Markus took their leave.

It had been a long day, and not entirely devoid of excitement, so I was more than ready for my bed. But before I said 'Good night,' I had to ask Holmes, 'Do you really suspect that Moriarty is involved, then?'

'Well, it is the sort of audacious scheme that one might expect of the professor. He may well have got on the trail in London – you recall that the king had rather foolishly employed some roughs to waylay Miss Adler, as she then was, before he employed my services. The professor, with his eyes and ears everywhere in the criminal underworld, may well have got his first hints then. Those whom the king employed may even have been Moriarty's men.'

'And the burglary in Paris, Holmes. I recollect your saying the last time I saw you that you suspected Moriarty of extending his operations to the Continent. It all fits together very neatly.'

'It does, Watson, although that does not prove that my theory, my suspicion, rather, is correct. But it is the most credible notion I can think of.'

'Again, though, I must ask if it gets us anywhere?'

'Oh, I think it does, or it will. If Moriarty is involved, then the local ruffians will be aware that there is a newcomer in their ranks, as it were, even though they may not know his identity. Moriarty has a way of making his presence felt. A few discreet enquiries among the shadier inhabitants of Dopzhe should –'

'Should get us a knife in the ribs, Holmes!'

He waved this minor point aside as irrelevant. 'I shall make it clear that we have no interest in their activities, but are merely seeking information about one of their competitors. They should welcome the chance to eliminate a rival, Watson!'

Not for the first time, I felt this was misreading the situation rather badly, but it is no use arguing with Holmes, so I gave a grunt and a nod that might be interpreted any way you chose, and said good night.

As I went out into the corridor to walk the few paces to my own bedroom, I reflected that it would have been so much simpler had we been able to arrange the meeting between Mrs Norton and the kidnappers, and follow the miscreants to their den. It was all very well for Holmes to theorize about Professor Moriarty, or for von Gratz to speak of anarchists, but they might both be wrong. And if they were right, anarchists are shy and retiring folk, not the sort of people to reveal their hiding places in a hurry; as for Moriarty, I knew that Holmes had been on his track for a couple of years now, without making any appreciable progress. What was the likelihood that our clumsy enquiries in the dives and dens of Dopzhe would produce anything other than that knife in the back of which I had made mention? No, if the photograph were not shattered, we could have observed the meeting, trailed the villain – *if* the photograph had not been smashed! 'If wishes were horses, then beggars would ride.' And unlucky beggars we were too, I thought. To have had the photograph in our hands, quite literally, and to lose it in so slapdash a manner. If only we still had that plate! Or again, if only we had thought to bring the fake plate along with us. As I have said, it was almost impossible to detect that it was a forgery, the tones being reversed; so that if Mrs Norton had the fake to show, the villains would be convinced, at least until such time as they could make a print and discover the truth. Time enough, at any rate, for Holmes and me to follow, to act.

I stopped dead, outside the door of my room. Fool that I was! I did not have the fake plate, it is true. But I knew where it was. It was in the safe, and I knew where the safe was, and I knew the very combination that would open it!

It was now late, almost two in the morning, our deliberations having dragged on somewhat. Gottfried and Karl, like more law-abiding citizens, would be in their beds asleep. Or they should be.

Why should they not? They would have seen the plundered bookcase, and assumed that we had been misled, outsmarted by a puerile trick stolen from Edgar Allan Poe! Yes, they would hastily check the safe, see that its contents were untouched, as they thought, have a stiff brandy and soda; exactly as you or I would do in the circumstances. Why should they not be sound asleep? And equally, why should I not return, commit a second burglary, and thereby save the day?

There was no need to tell Holmes, no need to trouble him. It was perfectly safe, I could see no danger at all in it. I still had the little dark lantern which Holmes had given me. I had thrown it on my bed when we first returned to the hotel, and there it was still. I went into my room, took the lantern and pushed it into a pocket, and found a scarf, hat and coat, all in two minutes or less. Then I was out in the corridor, and hastening as quickly and quietly as I could down the stairs.

The place, as you may imagine, given the lateness of the hour, was deserted. Only a sleepy concierge at the reception desk struggled to his feet, asking me, 'Is anything wrong, Monsieur?'

'Not at all,' I assured him. 'Can't sleep, a slight headache, a little fresh air, that's all,' and I went out into the dark and empty street.

There was a cab rank outside the hotel, but that too was empty save for one old fiacre whose driver sat slumped in his seat, asleep. I was obliged to climb up and shake him, and he looked at me with a good deal of resentment, until I showed him my purse and promised him double the usual fare. I told him to take me to the street wherein lay Gottfried's mansion – though I did not tell him the number – and we rattled off, with the concierge, evidently intrigued by these unwonted nocturnal activities, standing on the hotel steps staring after us and rubbing the sleep out of his eyes.

I got down from my carriage at the end of the street, waited until my driver had vanished from sight, then made my way down the mews at the back of the houses. The stable cottage was in darkness, and I tried the carriage gate and the postern door, but both were locked.

I wrapped my scarf about my face and pulled down my

hat, then I scrambled over the wall at the same spot as before, or very near. I pushed through the shrubbery, minced delicately across the lawn, and tried the windows. All were fastened, including the one which Holmes had opened earlier that evening, but that same one yielded to my penknife blade, and I was soon inside the house.

All was in darkness, and I lit my lantern but closed the shutter, so that only a narrow beam was thrown out. I made my way across the room, which seemed three or four times larger than I remembered, into the corridor, up the stairs.

Not until I reached the landing did I pause, and only then did the full enormity of my actions come to my fevered brain. What on earth was I thinking about, to commit burglary, and alone? Then I pulled myself together. I had come thus far undetected, unsuspected, I might as well play the man and see the thing through. I made my way to the door of the room that I knew to be Gottfried's bedroom. He would be in there, of course. Asleep, unless I were very unlucky, but still in there. But then need I go through the bedroom to reach the study? That was the way we had gone earlier, but I recollected that there was another door in the study, presumably leading to the corridor in which I now stood. If that were so, the study door should be the next one down. I moved to that door, tried it. It opened soundlessly, and I stepped inside and moved the beam of my lantern round.

As I had thought, I was in the study. Being careful not to trip up over low bookcases this time, I went to the section of bookshelf on the wall which concealed the safe. I moved the fake books, revealing the safe. I moved the shutter of my lantern to give a slightly more powerful beam, reached for the dial –

At that moment, the connecting door to the bedroom was thrown wide. The lights had been lit in there, and the broad beam of light fell full upon me as I lurked by the safe! I do not know what I ought to have done. I do know that I simply froze, stood there as if turned to stone.

Behind me, a voice said, 'Mr Sherlock Holmes, I presume?'

That broke the spell. I turned, bowed as best I could under the embarrassing circumstances, and replied, 'I fear that I cannot claim that honour, sir. I am Doctor John Watson, at your service.'

'Ah, yes.' The man at the door moved into the room, and I now saw firstly that he was holding a revolver, and secondly that another man stood behind him. The first man was the one whom von Gratz had pointed out as Duke Gottfried. The other one I did not know, but I took him to be Karl, the man I had seen muffled up outside the gate earlier; he had something of the appearance of the king about him, but a dissipated air which marred his looks.

'Duke Gottfried, is it not?' I said, with what nonchalance I could summon up. 'And this, if I am not mistaken, is Herr Karl-Heinz von Ormstein?'

Gottfried bowed. 'You are well informed, Doctor. As am I. You are known to us, sir, as Holmes's creature, his lackey. And doubtless you are here now at his bidding?'

'I resent the slur, sir! I am my own man, and I am here —'

Gottfried waved a hand, and laughed. 'I know very well why you are here,' he said. 'You entered this house earlier this evening, and took certain papers. Having discovered they were not what you sought — and I must congratulate you, or Holmes, rather, upon making that discovery so quickly, for they were excellent forgeries — having seen your mistake, Holmes sent you here, being afraid to come himself, to see if you could not do better a second time. Am I correct?'

I stood silent, unwilling to give him the satisfaction of provoking me. Then it occurred to me that I had a golden opportunity; I could still help Holmes, by convincing these villains that they were safe. That might not help Holmes find Mr Norton, and it would certainly not help me, for I strongly suspected that this precious pair intended to shoot me, and claim I was a burglar – which was true enough! But if they thought the genuine papers were still in their possession, they would leave Holmes alone, and thus if I could convince them that the papers were still in the safe, I should have removed one potential source of trouble. I let my shoulders slump, and muttered dispiritedly, 'You are right, damn you! Right in every particular. Damn you, and damn Holmes, for getting me into this.'

'You are out of your depth,' Karl told me, not unkindly. 'Look at that safe.' I did so. 'Do you know how many possible combinations of letters are possible? It is astronomical.'

And Gottfried put in, with a sort of forced carelessness, 'And even were you to open the safe, the papers you seek are no longer there. I moved them when I knew you had been in the house.'

'What are we to do with this fellow?' asked Karl.

'Oh, let him go.' It was, of course, Gottfried who said this, but he echoed my own sentiments to perfection! My spirits rose a little. Gottfried went on, 'We have nothing to fear now. Doctor, my servants will – ah, show you out. You will please to tell Mr Holmes not to call upon me again, for it will be useless.' And he touched a bell by the door.

A couple of minutes later a butler arrived, tucking his shirt into his trousers and looking rather flustered. 'Ah,' said Gottfried, 'would you fetch Hans and Fritz, and escort this gentleman out?'

And the butler went off, to return shortly with a couple of sturdy footmen, both looking very sleepy and both looking very displeased at being woken from their slumbers. They evidently sensed that I was the indirect cause of their disturbed night's rest, and they handled me none too gently as a consequence, frog-marching me down the stairs, along the corridor, down the drive, and – after the butler had made a great show of unlocking the main gate – pitching me headlong into the gutter.

The butler made a few irrelevant remarks as I lay there, and the footmen too did not hesitate to give me their own opinions as to my appearance, ancestry and future prospects.

As I stood up and dusted myself down, the trio wandered back to the house and their beds, and all I could do was stand there watching them.

'Well, Watson,' I told myself out loud, 'a pretty botch you have made of this, and not for the first time!'

'It is the truth,' said a well-known voice from the shadows. 'But what exactly is it that you have made a botch of?'

'Is that you, Holmes? You ought not end a sentence with a preposition, you know,' was the best I could do for response.

Holmes emerged from the shadow and laughed. 'But seriously, what have you been up to?' he asked, regarding me closely under the street lamp. 'Not some notion of stealing the fake plate, was it?'

'Why, yes, Holmes! I thought –'

'You thought that we could give it to Mrs Norton, and

she could give it to the villain, thereby allaying his suspicions for long enough to allow us to follow him?'

'Just so.' I gazed ruefully at my dusty boots. 'It seemed a rather good idea at the time.'

'Oh, the idea was good enough. It was merely the execution which – ah, fell short.'

'Indeed. Still, I have made them think that we really do want what is in the safe, and thus convinced them that it is genuine.'

'That is something, I suppose.'

'But how did you know I was here, Holmes?'

'I heard you sneak out of the hotel. Or rather I heard you moving about, making enough noise for a herd of elephants, and then leave your room, and I was curious, so I followed you. But I had to change first, for even here in Bohemia I am not quite so Bohemian as to wander the streets in my night-shirt. So by the time I got down to the lobby you had taken your cab, and there was not another on the rank, and I had to follow much of the way on foot. Fortunately the concierge had overheard you tell the address to the driver, and I knew immediately that you proposed to break in. I could not, for a moment, think why; but then I realized what you intended. It was a clever scheme, and I must congratulate you upon it.'

'Are you joking?'

'Far from it. I only wish you had spoken to me, for this little contretemps might have been avoided.'

'You mean you would have broken in yourself, and not been detected?' I asked.

'Not a bit of it. I should not have broken in at all.'

'But then how would you get hold of the fake plate?'

'I would not have done so,' said Holmes calmly.

'But –'

'We do not need the fake plate. Or rather, we do not need *that* fake plate.'

I stared at him. 'But – oh! You mean that we could simply have faked our own?'

Holmes nodded. 'A couple of actors, the right costume, and the thing is done. Von Gratz is an expert photographer, he would take it for us. We shall do it tomorrow, and Mrs Norton can place her advertisement at the same time.'

'So that all this –' I stopped, and stared at him.

'Just so, Watson.' He started to laugh, and after a moment or so I joined in.

NINE

Holmes made a couple of minor changes to our original plan. The first was that on our return he spoke to the concierge at the Albion, asking him to place an advertisement in such of the morning papers as could be contacted at that ungodly hour, on the lines of 'Irene assures Papa that all is well, and asks for a meeting as soon as possible,' if I recall correctly. 'The sooner the better,' he told me. 'The newspapers print their morning editions through the night, and we may be able to get the message into enough of them to do the trick. And then we must make plans to acquire our own forged plate.'

'Let's just hope they do not make their own print before we have found Norton,' I said.

Holmes answered, 'I have hopes that we shall find him quickly. But even if we do not, there is no reason why they should wish to make a print, at least until the King of Scandinavia is here in Bohemia. In any case, we shall give them the print which we took from Gottfried, and the one which Mrs Norton has already. Why should they need a third?'

I frowned at this. 'Are we not running a risk, giving them the prints?'

'Not at all,' said Holmes, yawning. 'As someone said at the outset, the prints might easily have been faked. No, without the original plate, there is little danger.' He smiled. 'Indeed, it might be rather amusing to challenge them to produce the plate, and make a print from it in front of reliable witnesses! That would tend to prove the suggestion that all the prints were faked.'

'Well, if you are sure.'

'I am certain.' He yawned again, and glanced at his watch. 'Dear me! It is later than I thought, and I am quite sleepy. It might be as well to get what rest we can, for we may be somewhat busy tomorrow – or later today, rather.'

On that note we went to our respective rooms. I do not know about Holmes, but I slept like the proverbial log, not waking until almost ten that morning. Holmes had already breakfasted when I got down to the dining room, and he frowned and checked his watch. 'The advertisement is here,' he said, waving a newspaper at me.

'What, the reply?' I fear that I was still not fully awake.

'Not the reply! Our original advertisement, the concierge succeeded in getting it into this morning's edition. Now we must wait for the reply.'

I groaned inwardly, for I knew that Holmes frets abominably when he is obliged to wait for anything of that kind. I told him, 'We have another task, though. We must get the fake photograph made, and quickly, for the reply may be in the evening paper, and the meeting might be tonight. We need a fake to show them.'

He brightened up somewhat at this, and outlined his second modification to the original plan. 'I have decided that there is no need to hire actors,' he told me. 'It will be much safer, lead to less gossip, if we do the entire job ourselves.'

I demurred slightly, but he insisted, and, instead of

hiring actors for the photograph, Holmes and I took the parts ourselves! Von Gratz had a studio of sorts in his rooms, complete with a painted canvas backdrop depicting a country scene, and we sat before that, whilst von Gratz busied himself with camera and magnesium flare. I flatter myself that I did a reasonable job of masquerading as the king, while Holmes was able to indulge his taste for female impersonation, a taste which I try to discourage whenever possible, but which did seem justified in this instance.

I must say that the finished plate would have fooled me, though of course the print which von Gratz made from it gave the game away at once, and I reiterated my hope that the villains would not make a print from it to verify its authenticity. Holmes, as before, waved this aside.

The actual process of posing for the photograph and its subsequent development took up much of the afternoon, so that when we emerged, blinking even in the watery sunlight after the darkness of studio and darkroom and the flash of the magnesium, the afternoon papers were out. Holmes eagerly attacked the nearest news vendor, and bought a copy of all the titles he had.

'It is here!' he cried. '"Irene – meet Papa at the Café Florian at eight. Come alone". The Café Florian?' he asked von Gratz.

'A low place with an unwholesome reputation, much frequented by the ladies of the town, by writers and similar scum. Oh, I beg your pardon, Doctor!'

'Not at all,' said I, being accustomed to that sort of thing. 'And for disguises?'

'Oh, if we are to be writers, any shabby and unfashionable old rags will do.'

We had spoken to Mrs Norton earlier that day to tell her

of our plans – indeed, it was one of her old dresses which Holmes had worn for the photograph. Needless to say, she had heard our news with delight, and was eager to do whatever she could to help. 'Which is little enough,' said Holmes, when we had sought her out again. 'Simply to take the papers along, meet whoever turns up, and listen to what he or she has to say. Now, it may be that you will be told where to find your husband, or asked to go with the person who contacts you. In that case, you will say that you mistrust them, and need to bring two friends to ensure that there is no treachery. You understand that?'

'Perfectly.'

'But I do not think that is likely,' Holmes went on. 'The likelihood is that they will wish to check the papers first, before they release Mr Norton. In that event, they will take the papers and leave, telling you to wait for further instructions. I repeat, that is the most likely thing. If I am right, you will do nothing, do not attempt to follow, but merely return to your hotel.'

Mrs Norton nodded. 'I understand, Mr Holmes.'

'Here are the papers,' said Holmes, handing over a neat package. 'The original letters, two photographic prints, genuine, one glass plate, not quite so genuine, but the villains will not know that.'

I hoped he was right, but I did not voice my doubts a third time. Mrs Norton, brave woman though she was, should not be troubled just now, when we were relying upon her.

We all dined together, Holmes, Mrs Norton, von Gratz, Markus and myself. We were a sombre enough party, for I think we all had a sense of how important was the task ahead of us, with a man's life as the prize. Holmes, as usual, ate almost nothing, and for once I did not press him; he has his little ways, as do we all, and I did not want to make the gathering any gloomier than it already was.

At last it was time for Holmes to set off. The plan was this: Holmes, suitably disguised as a lounger, was to go alone to the café twenty minutes before the appointed time. Then Mrs Norton and Markus, in a closed carriage with the blinds drawn down, would follow; the carriage being closed, and the presence of Markus, would, we trusted, discourage any attempt at recovering the package before they arrived at the café. As a further precaution, von Gratz would follow in a second carriage, under orders to prevent any attack on the first.

Meantime I would be in yet a third carriage, a little way down the street from the café. Mrs Norton would get down alone from her carriage, and Markus would drive off, while von Gratz would also drive past the café quite innocently. They would leave their carriages when once they were out of sight, and attempt to rejoin me.

The object of all this rigmarole was firstly to ensure that Mrs Norton was not waylaid and the plate stolen before Holmes could spot the person meeting Mrs Norton; and secondly that only Holmes did the actual following of that person, while the rest of us followed Holmes, at a safe distance. Holmes himself had insisted on this second point, saying that he could guarantee to remain unobserved himself, but could not answer for the rest of us. We let this slur pass, feeling that we might all of us in any event be glad of a carriage – should the villain take a cab, let us say, and there not be another handy.

I was at my appointed station, far enough from the café to allay suspicion, five minutes before time. I studied the place, cramped and looking none too clean from where I sat, for some time before I recognized Holmes, and that despite the fact that I knew what he looked like in his disguise. In some mysterious way he could assume not merely the outward appearance, but the very nature of the person he sought to portray; I never saw a more perfect specimen of a drunken and aggressive ruffian in my life, and I noticed that the other customers, riff-raff though they were, took some pains to avoid him.

Mrs Norton's carriage swept up to the café, as out of place there as an orchid in a cabbage patch, and even from where I sat I could hear a chorus of ribald comments as she descended; a chorus in which Holmes's own voice joined loudly with a lack of shame and grammar alike.

Mrs Norton ignored them all, and sat by herself at a tiny table. Her carriage rattled off, leaving her there, and another, that I knew contained von Gratz, also went past. Mrs Norton sat there, sipping a coffee, for some ten minutes, during which time both Markus and von Gratz joined me in my cab.

'Anything?' asked von Gratz, as he climbed in.

'Nothing,' I said, shaking my head. 'I see that all went well with you.'

'H'mm,' said von Gratz.

'Did it not?'

'Well, there was no attempt made upon us,' said von Gratz, 'but I could have sworn that someone followed us.'

'Ah! Did you think so?' I asked Markus.

'Frankly, sir, I did not,' said Markus, with a hint of embarrassment in his voice, which I read as meaning that he thought von Gratz was being fanciful, but dare not say as much before his superior officer. With palpable relief he tapped my arm and pointed. 'That may be the fellow,' he said.

A lounger, very nearly as ill-dressed and dirty as Holmes himself, and that is saying a lot, had detached himself from the shadows and joined Mrs Norton at her table. There was a brief discussion, as it seemed, and then Mrs Norton handed over the little package, and the man stood up and left the café, heading for us in our cab.

We studiously avoided looking at him as he passed us, but instead we engaged in some boisterously loud discussion of the latest play. I saw Holmes flit by, then I waited a moment before looking discreetly through the rear window. I saw our man halt at the end of the road and look back. He could not suspect us in the cab, we were so obviously pointed the wrong way; and there was not the slightest sign of Holmes, though I knew that he must be somewhere in my field of view.

The man turned to the left, and vanished. I fancied that I saw Holmes follow, but I could not be sure. Then it was time to turn the cab round and start to follow on our own account.

We went slowly back the way we had come, and turned left. I could just make out Holmes, dodging from shadow to shadow, and I told the driver to follow, but as slowly as may be. At the end of that road he turned right, and I told the driver to speed up to the turning. I spotted Holmes again, this time getting into a cab. 'Follow that fiacre,' I told our driver,' and don't lose him.'

We rattled along at a smarter pace now, keeping Holmes's cab just in view, slowing when he slowed in response to the quarry, though these pauses were infrequent – evidently our man did not suspect that he was being followed.

Curiously enough, I did. Whether what von Gratz had said earlier had preyed upon my mind, or whether the cause was something entirely different, I cannot say. Yet I found myself turning round to look behind more than once; and, of course, there was nobody to be seen, nothing at all out of the way.

At last Holmes's cab stopped, and he got down, waved to us, and set off on foot at a fair speed. We moved to close up with him, then the driver grunted something, and I looked to see Holmes making his way through a narrow court where the cab could not follow.

'Stop here!' I cried to the driver. And I told von Gratz and Markus, 'I'll follow on foot, and you do what you can.'

Markus told us, 'That alley leads to the Boulevard Vitosha, unless I am much mistaken.'

'Then you take the cab there, and we shall try to meet shortly,' I said, getting out of the cab. I hurried across the road and into the alley. As soon as I entered it, I spied Holmes at the further end, loitering and evidently watching to see where our quarry went.

I hastened along the alley, and caught up with him. 'Well?'

'Ah, Watson. Our man has just crossed the street here, and dodged into a stately mansion.'

'But he was dressed in a very down-at-heel manner, Holmes. I thought he must be an anarchist.' I stared where Holmes pointed, to see what was indeed a 'stately mansion', set well back from the tree-lined boulevard in its own spacious and well-kept grounds. 'Not exactly what I'd call an anarchists' den, is it?'

'Indeed not, Watson. I fear we must abandon that particular theory.'

'In favour of the premise that Moriarty is behind the abduction of Mr Norton?'

'I still do not rule out that possibility,' said Holmes calmly. 'Ah, here are our allies,' and he nodded to where the cab had just come round the corner and into the street.

We crossed to the cab as it pulled up, and climbed inside. Holmes nodded to the house, saying, 'Our man has just gone in there. We must find out the identity of the owner, and as soon as possible.'

Von Gratz laughed. 'That is easily done,' he told us. 'That is the town house of Count Maurice von Ormstein.'

TEN

'I see,' said Holmes, drumming his fingers on the window of the carriage.

I was just about to ask who this Maurice von Ormstein might be, when I recollected that I had heard the name before. 'The king's cousin?' I said. 'And not Professor Moriarty, then?' I added in an undertone.

Holmes clicked his tongue impatiently, for he hates to be proved wrong.

'A distant cousin,' said von Gratz, referring to Maurice. 'A soldier, like us, and very popular with the army, much of which would support him in any struggle for power.'

'But,' added Markus, 'his claim to the throne is so tenuous, his line is so distant from that of the king, that there would be trouble if Maurice tried to take power.'

'It is true,' said von Gratz. 'I have said that much of the army would support him; but only if the present king were not on the throne, for the first allegiance of the army is to Wilhelm. And even if Wilhelm died, or abdicated, by no means all the army would support Maurice. And that is not to speak of Gottfried's own party! We may have spiked Gottfried's guns as far as the papers and the photograph are concerned, but he would undoubtedly cast his hat into the ring if the throne were to become vacant. And Gottfried's claim, so far as birth and ancestry go, is far stronger than that of Maurice.' He frowned. 'I must confess that I have met Maurice once or twice, and I never detected any sort of overweening ambition in the man.'

Markus said, 'Forgive me, Colonel, but I cannot entirely agree.'

'Oh?'

'I recall one occasion, when we – some of the junior officers, that is to say – were making merry, and the champagne flowed freely, this Maurice let slip some hint that he would not be entirely averse to the notion of high office, perhaps even to a crown. At the time, of course, I thought it was merely the wine talking. And then he is a nobleman, with a distant connection to the royal house. So all in all, it was the sort of thing anyone might say under the circumstances. Now, though, I wonder if perhaps the mask had not slipped just a little?'

'Or perhaps,' I suggested, with a sidelong glance at Holmes, 'perhaps he has been put up to it by some outside agency?'

Von Gratz and Markus looked puzzled, but Holmes laughed. 'I do not rule out the possibility,' he told me. 'However, the immediate question is just this – what is our next action to be?'

'A direct attack,' said von Gratz at once. 'We are acquaintances of his, Markus and I, so why cannot we simply knock on his door, say we were passing and decided to look in?'

'He is hardly likely to greet us with the news that he is holding Mr Norton prisoner!' said Markus.

'True, but then we shall observe how he reacts to seeing us upon his doorstep,' said von Gratz. 'If he gives a guilty start, if he fails to ask us in – would that not be a pointer?'

'You may be right,' said Holmes. 'Watson and I will remain here, for we do not wish to show our hand too soon.

Your involvement in this matter is not yet known, gentlemen, or not to anyone save Gottfried and Karl, and if this Maurice is their rival we may assume that they have not informed him! So we rely upon you to play the part of good comrades who have called upon him quite by accident.'

Von Gratz and Markus undertook to play their part, got down from the cab and strolled to the door. We could just make out the liveried footman who opened it to them, then they went inside.

'And who ever heard of a young soldier employing a footman?' I mused.

'I suppose some of the great men of the past,' said Holmes. 'Wellington, probably? Napoleon?'

'Exactly. Men with ambition, Holmes! I think we may be on the right track now.'

'And you would not bet that Moriarty is not inside that house?' he asked with a smile.

'I would bet —' and I paused. 'No, Holmes. I shall not take your money!'

He laughed again. 'Perhaps I do see Moriarty every-where, Watson. One day I shall have to tackle him, and soon, I think. I am accumulating my proofs, my evidence. But this Maurice, with his grand house and his servants, does indeed seem the man we seek for the present, without looking further.'

'Or one of the men, for if this Karl and Gottfried dis-cover our imposition, they may turn nasty.'

'H'mm. I see little immediate danger there, Watson. They cannot now hope to secure the throne for themselves, so there remains only revenge for our spoiling their sport.'

'Revenge is a powerful engine, Holmes. Drives men to all sorts of nastiness.'

'We shall keep a watchful eye open,' said Holmes. And he glanced at his watch. 'But for the present, we can only hope that our friends keep their eyes open.'

As I have said earlier, Holmes can be somewhat fidgety when he is waiting for things to happen, especially when it is a question of relying upon others to accomplish the desired object. On this occasion, though, he sank back in deep thought, and it was I who began, after an hour or so, to wonder just when the other two would return with news of some sort or other. Another half hour, and the strain began to be well-nigh intolerable; when two hours were up, I felt that I could stand it no longer. I had almost decided to get down and stretch my legs, if I could do nothing else, when the front door of the house opened and von Gratz and Markus emerged, to stand at the door deep in conversation with a third man whom I did not recognize, but took to be Maurice von Ormstein. He was some twenty years of age, tall, not unlike the king himself to look at, as I could see by the light that came from inside the house.

'At last!' muttered Holmes, at my side.

'I thought you were asleep.'

He laughed. 'Merely possessing my soul in what patience I could muster, Watson. That, and trying to work out just how the various characters fit into our little drama. Mrs Norton, her husband, Gottfried, Karl, and now this fellow Maurice, whom we had not hitherto even considered.'

I could not refrain from asking, 'And Professor Moriarty?'

Holmes laughed. 'Well, perhaps we may eliminate him from our enquiries for the time being. But the relations, or possible relations, between the others are interesting.'

'I don't see why,' I said. Surely Mrs Norton is only

involved because her husband has been kidnapped? And Mr Norton's part is even simpler!'

'Is it?'

'Isn't it?'

'Well, suppose that Godfrey Norton is indeed a "guest" of this fellow Maurice. He need not be an unwilling guest, need he?'

'You mean the two of them could be in it together?'

'You put the argument succinctly, Watson, and with that command of literary fluency which marks you as a writer. Yes, my boy, the two of them could indeed be in it together, the abduction might have been as fake as the photograph we have just passed to Maurice's agent.'

'But why on earth should Norton fake his own kidnapping?' I asked. 'After all, if he wanted to acquire the papers, he could simply take them from wherever his wife had put them.'

'Could he, though? Perhaps Mrs Norton did not reveal her choice of hiding place even to her husband? Or perhaps he thought that they were safe enough, but then this Karl stole them, and Norton had to get them back?'

'Doesn't make sense, Holmes! Assuming that Norton did – for whatever reason – want the papers back after Karl had stolen them, why should he not simply put the matter to Mrs Norton, ask her to ask you to help?'

'Perhaps he dare not do so?' said Holmes. 'Did you never have the least suspicion of Norton back in London, a year or so ago, when the king first consulted me?'

'I did think the Nortons' wedding was a touch odd,' I replied. 'Hastily arranged, that sort of thing.'

'My first suspicion was that Norton was himself a paid agent, hired to ensure that the papers were never used against the king, or perhaps to acquire the papers for some third party.'

'Moriarty?'

'I did not say so.'

'You know what occurred to me, Holmes?'

'No.'

'The coincidence of names. Godfrey; Gottfried. Wondered if it might be the same man? No, I suppose not. Mrs Norton knew Gottfried. Or did she? I can't recall if she said, and anyway she told us so many lies that we just couldn't be certain.'

Holmes laughed. 'Our client was not absolutely honest with us at the start of our investigations, it is true. And yet I think we have not done too badly, save for the actual recovery of Mr Norton, and the returning of him to his wife.' He nodded through the carriage window. 'And perhaps we may tidy up those last loose ends. They are returning, so we should have some answers soon, and we can possibly look forward to completing the case in a satisfactory fashion.'

Von Gratz and Markus climbed into the carriage, and we set off back towards the Albion Hotel. 'Well?' asked Holmes at once.

Von Gratz gave a shrug. 'He asked us in readily enough, and seemed at his ease.'

'No sign of guilt, of wanting to avoid you?'

'None.'

'And no sign of the man whom we followed to the house?'

'None,' repeated von Gratz.

'And yet the papers were there, on his desk,' Markus put in.

'What? I never saw them,' said von Gratz.

'You recall that I wandered about the room?' said Markus. 'I picked up a book here and there, glanced at his pictures. I could not of course, actually rifle through the papers and so forth on his desk, but I took particular notice of what was there. The package which Mrs Norton had earlier was there, under some letters and what have you. I could not mention it to the colonel, obviously.'

'Well done,' said von Gratz. 'And now, Mr Holmes? Do we get a squadron of lancers, return and arrest the fellow?'

'That rather depends upon whether Mr Norton is in the house,' said Holmes.

'He is not,' said Markus at once.

'And how can you know that?'

'I mentioned that I had leave of absence from my regiment – the colonel very kindly substantiated my untruth –'

'For the purpose of maintaining the deception only,' added von Gratz with a laugh.

Markus went on, 'I said that I planned to spend some weeks in the capital, myself and a couple of other officers, devoting ourselves to riotous living. Maurice at once offered us the run of his town house. Now, he would hardly want three or four officers in the place if he had a prisoner tucked away there, would he?'

'It seems unlikely,' Holmes agreed.

'In any event,' said von Gratz, 'it is quite unnecessary to keep Norton here in the capital. Maurice, if he plans to blackmail the king, must be here, where the palace is; and the papers must be here, too, to reinforce the threat. But Norton is not a key part of the main scheme. He is, or was, needed only to help Maurice acquire the papers, and thus he might be hidden away anywhere.'

'That is quite true. But it scarcely helps us,' said Holmes.

'It may not be as bad as it seems, though,' said Markus. 'Maurice has an estate in the country, miles from anywhere. Just the place to keep a man prisoner, for no-one but Maurice's own servants go near the place.'

'Ahah!' said Holmes, sitting up. 'That sounds the very place we are seeking. How do we reach this estate? And how soon can we get there?'

'A train to Saltzenbach, then a cab,' said Markus. 'That is quicker than taking a carriage the whole way.'

'Horses?' asked von Gratz, like a true cavalryman.

Markus shook his head. 'The way is through forests and mountains, Colonel. An express will outrun a horse in that country.'

'And when is the next express?' asked Holmes.

Von Gratz shook his head, and looked at Markus, who said, 'I do not think there will be another tonight. Early tomorrow morning? I am afraid I do not know the precise times, but the manager at the hotel –' and he pointed out of the carriage window, to show that we were now approaching the Albion – 'should have a time-table.'

We rushed into the hotel in a body, and Holmes asked the startled concierge, 'Have you a railway time-table?'

'Why, yes, sir. A moment, if you please, and I shall bring one to you. Oh, sir,' he added, as he turned away, 'there is a lady to see you. In the smaller sitting room.' And he pointed the way.

Holmes glanced at me and raised an eyebrow.

'Mrs Norton?' I hazarded. 'It surely cannot be anyone else.'

My guess was correct. The small sitting room, little more than an alcove, but entirely private, being well out of the run of the everyday business of the hotel, had only one occupant. Mrs Norton rose to greet us as we entered, and her first words were, 'Have you found him? Godfrey, I mean? You followed that dreadful man, and you would not return had you failed, so you must have found him?'

'We have hopes that your husband may be recovered shortly,' Holmes told her.

Mrs Norton's face showed bitter disappointment. 'I had hoped that he would be with you,' she said. 'You have been gone so long, that I thought –'

'We believe that we know his whereabouts,' said Holmes, in his most soothing tone.

'Oh? And where is he?'

Holmes hesitated – even under those circumstances, he hesitated! His innate reluctance to reveal information prevented his acting like any ordinary man.

I said, 'We think he is held at the country estate of Maurice von Ormstein.'

'Oh! Maurice? Are you sure?'

'We cannot be absolutely certain, madam,' said Holmes, glancing at me with some annoyance – quite unjustified annoyance, if you ask me – 'but we shall take the first available train, and test our theory.'

At that moment, the concierge entered the room, bearing a small fat book. 'The time-table, sir,' he said.

Holmes snatched the little volume from him, and riffled through it. He found the page he sought, read eagerly, then looked up with some exasperation. 'The first direct train is not until eight, and that is not an express. The first express is not until after nine.'

'That will permit us to get a decent night's sleep, start refreshed, then,' I said.

But Mrs Norton cried, 'Surely not! We must go at once,

if there is the slightest chance of rescuing Godfrey. Can we not hire a special train? I shall pay for it myself.'

'No need, madam,' said von Gratz. 'We can do even better than a special, I fancy.'

'How so?' asked Holmes.

'The royal train,' said von Gratz. 'It is kept in readiness for His Majesty, whenever he might need it. I can telegraph from here, and it should take no more than an hour to prepare the engine. That gives us time to arm ourselves, and pack what necessities we may need.'

'That is capital,' said Holmes. 'You telegraph, Colonel, and we may leave immediately, I fancy, for we have no need of elaborate preparations.'

'Indeed not,' said Mrs Norton, as von Gratz made to leave the room. 'Although I do wish that I had brought my old "walking-clothes" with me, for the current fashion is not exactly conducive to ease of movement,' and she looked down ruefully at her long and elaborate dress.

I knew that by 'walking-clothes' she meant the masculine attire which she had adopted as a disguise in the case which first brought her to our attention, some time previously; but other than that I had not the least idea as to what she meant to convey.

Holmes, however, was quicker than I. 'You surely do not mean that you wished to accompany us, madam?'

'And you surely do not mean that you wish me to remain, sir?'

'But – the danger! And –'

'What is that to me?' asked Mrs Norton. 'A wife's place is by her husband's side, especially when that husband is himself in trouble or danger.'

'It is only fair, Holmes,' I put in.

He shot me a venomous look, then his face cleared. 'Perhaps you are right, after all,' he said. 'But you must undertake not to interfere, madam.'

'Oh, I am not one of those who see the roles of men and women as perfectly interchangeable,' said Mrs Norton. And she said it with a little laugh that probably fooled Holmes, but would not have fooled me, or any other married man!

Holmes mumbled something or the other, then asked me in a loud voice, 'Have you your revolver, Watson?'

I all but groaned aloud at this pitiful attempt to convince Mrs Norton of the dangers of the projected enterprise, and answered him, 'Yes, Holmes, I have it, and a couple of boxes of cartridges.' At which he subsided into a sulky silence, cheering up only when von Gratz returned to say that he had telegraphed to the station, and all was arranged.

A short cab ride brought us to the railway station, and a very deferential station master escorted us to the platform where the royal train stood waiting. We had a slight delay, for no train, even a royal one, can be made ready literally 'upon a moment's notice.' The engine must still be fired up, and what have you – my vagueness here reflects my ignorance of the technical procedures – but the delay was not by any means as lengthy as might have been expected. I rather fancy that the 'royal' appellation referred only to the carriages, which were indeed luxuriously, royally, appointed, and that the engine was simply the first that was more or less fired up and could be moved, but I cannot be sure. In any event, some twenty minutes after our arrival at the station, we were able to settle back into the leather seats and doze off, as the train raced through the night bound for the little country town of Saltzenbach.

ELEVEN

The town of Saltzenbach lies in a fold of a mountain range which is, I think, a northern and western offshoot of the distant Carpathians. I understand that the town was originally a prosperous place, its wealth coming from the salt mines implied in the name, but it now bears the same air of faded grandeur and neglect which characterizes much of Bohemia, and these days the place largely depends upon seasonal visitors for its continued existence.

This is mostly hearsay, for the railway station is a short distance outside the town, and then it was still only early in the morning when the train pulled up, so that my first-hand observations were necessarily fleeting. We found a cab outside the station, and von Gratz asked if the driver knew the country estate of Maurice von Ormstein.

'Count's hunting lodge, you mean, sir?'

'That is the place. You know it?'

'Yes, sir.' The driver hesitated. 'Fair old drive, sir. Six or seven miles.'

'No matter, we shall pay whatever it costs.'

'And the count's not there just at the moment, sir,' said the driver, with an admirable reluctance to take our money under false pretences.

'No,' Holmes put in, 'we are to await him there. That reminds me, I am not sure if he sent word to his people to expect us. I don't suppose there is a telegraph to the hunting lodge, is there?'

'Bless you, sir, no such thing,' said the driver.

'So no means of getting a message to there quickly?'

The driver smiled. 'Well, sir, the count usually telegraphs here, to the station – there's a telegraph here, you see – and the station master he would ask me, or one of my mates, to drive to the lodge with the message. That way, we don't lose too much time, see?'

'Yes, I see. An admirable arrangement. You would not happen to know if any message was received and forwarded last night, I suppose?'

'There wasn't, sir. I've been there all night, more or less, and the station master would've come and asked me to drive up there, had he received a telegram.' The driver looked at Holmes anxiously. 'They might not expect you then, sir?'

'No matter,' said Holmes. 'We shall announce ourselves, for it is as quick for you to take us as it would be for you to take a message!'

'True enough,' said the driver.

'Be so good as to tell me when we are almost there,' said Holmes.

'Very good, sir.' And the driver shook the reins to start his horse off.

In a lower tone, Holmes told us, 'That is excellent. Maurice has evidently not yet examined the plate closely, or made another print from it.'

'No reason why he should,' I said, 'unless he suspected Mrs Norton here of treachery, and the fact that he has her husband will make him inclined to rule out that possibility. As you told the driver, Holmes, we shall announce ourselves.' And I took out my revolver and checked its cylinder.

We drove on in silence through the forest for an hour or so, and it was growing properly light, when the driver slowed down and called to Holmes, 'Begging your pardon, sir, but you asked me to let you know when we were nearly there?'

'I did, and thank you. Stop, if you would. Now, how far away are we, and where is the lodge from here?'

The driver pointed with his whip to a bend in the road, which here was little more than a track through the trees. 'Just follow the road, sir. Five minutes' walk. Shall I go on?'

'No, I have a fancy to continue on foot,' said Holmes. 'Wait here for us. The lady will stay here, too. Just until we make sure that they are expecting us,' he added, in an attempt to explain this odd behaviour.

The driver shrugged, as much as to say that all the gentry were mad, and the English gentry were perhaps the maddest of all, but that, so long as his fare were paid, their madness was of no consequence to him.

Holmes strolled along as if he were taking a walk before breakfast, but as soon as we turned the corner and could no longer be seen from the cab, he dived into the trees, and the rest of us followed him.

'We must approach quietly,' he told us, 'for these villains might have orders to harm Mr Norton in the event that the house is stormed.'

'Then what is our best course?' asked Markus.

'To approach the place unobserved, and spy out the land.' And Holmes set off through the trees before we could ask any more questions.

The hunting lodge was built of timber, great logs split in two, and it was on a grand scale – I fancy there must have been ten or a dozen bedrooms in it. The forest came pretty close to it, so we quite easily got within a dozen feet of the house. There was no sort of garden round it, but there was a little range of outbuildings, one of which was evidently a hen house put there to provide the lodge's owner with his breakfast eggs, for we could hear the birds scratching and cackling, and an aggressive cockerel strutted about on the path before the front door.

As we lurked in the trees just behind this hen house, trying to work out our best course of action, the front door of the lodge opened, and an old fellow came slowly out. He must have been seventy years old, perhaps more, and he had a sort of canvas sack in his hand. He came towards us, and we crouched lower in our hiding place. But the old chap was merely attending to the hens, throwing handfuls of corn or some similar fodder to the cockerel, then scrabbling in the little hut for the eggs. As he moved round towards us, Holmes stood up, threw an arm round the old fellow's neck, and pulled him into the cover of the trees.

'No need to be alarmed,' said Holmes. 'We have no quarrel with you.'

The old fellow mumbled something in the local dialect.

Holmes repeated his assurance in German, and the old man replied in the same language, but with a thick accent, 'I knew no good would come of it!'

'Did you, indeed?'

'I did. Fifty years and more I've worked for the count's family. Man and boy. And my father before me. And I never knew anything like this, not in all that time. Nor my father neither. Turn in his grave, he would, if he was alive to see this, and the old count would do the same.'

Without bothering to debate the logical paradox, Holmes asked, 'And what exactly is going on here?'

'Them fellows.' This was said with a good deal of contempt, and then he unbent sufficiently to add, 'And that other poor chap, that they're keeping locked up. Never known such a thing.'

'That is why we are here,' said Holmes. 'We are here to rescue the poor man who is locked up.'

'I dunno,' said the aged retainer doubtfully. 'I mean, the count himself said it was all right.'

'But you know better,' said Holmes. 'After all, there has never been anything like this in fifty years, has there? Certainly not in the old count's day.'

'That's right enough.'

'And what would your father say?'

'Oh, he'd have plenty to say! Knew his mind, my old man, and not afraid to speak it. Nor to use his fists, neither.'

'There you are, then,' said Holmes persuasively.

'Well –'

'And we are not asking you to run any great risk,' added Holmes, 'but merely to return to the lodge, and let us follow you inside. What do you say?'

'I'll do it!'

'Capital! How many of them are in there?'

'Three. Four, with the fellow who's locked up.'

'Very well. Just say and do whatever you would normally say and do, and leave the rest to us.'

The old man nodded. We checked our pistols, and the old man led the way to the door, pushed it open and stepped inside, while Holmes and the rest of us followed cautiously.

From somewhere inside, a voice called in German, 'Is that you, Jakob?'

'Who else would it be? Got some nice eggs here.'

'You took your time –' and the speaker, a short man with a ruffianly aspect, broke off as he came into the room and saw us.

Holmes immediately put his revolver to the man's head. 'I shall not hesitate to shoot,' he told him. 'Where are the other two?'

The man pointed to a door. 'In there.'

'Watson, you keep an eye on this fellow. And you – Jakob, is it? – could you find some rope to secure our prisoners?' Holmes nodded to von Gratz and Markus. 'Ready, gentlemen?'

They signified assent, and whilst I levelled my revolver at the first villain, Holmes threw open the door and burst into the next room, followed closely by the others. I heard an exclamation of surprise, an angry curse, then the sounds of a scuffle. A moment after, Holmes emerged, a look of triumph on his face.

'Now,' he asked the man whom I was watching, 'where is Mr Godfrey Norton?'

'Find out, if you're so clever!'

Holmes shrugged, and nodded to old Jakob, who had appeared with a length of rope. 'Tie this fellow up, would you? And the other two as well. Watson, we must search the house.'

We tried a couple of rooms, before finding a door which was locked. Holmes started back to search our prisoners for the key, but by this time von Gratz and Markus had joined us, and Markus gave the door a single glance, then raised his boot and simply kicked it in.

'It would have been the work of moment to find the key, and thus do no damage,' said Holmes mildly. To which Markus replied that damaging the property of a kidnapper and traitor did not weigh heavily upon his conscience.

We entered the room, and found it occupied by a man who sat tied to a chair. Holmes quickly cut the ropes which bound him, and asked, 'Mr Godfrey Norton?'

'I am, sir. And who may I thank for this timely rescue?'

'I am Sherlock Holmes, and –'

'Ah! I have heard of you, Mr Holmes, from my wife. And this, I take it, is Doctor Watson? I am delighted to meet you, sir.' Godfrey Norton was a tall young man, handsome, and with a firm handshake, although his face bore signs of his recent ordeal.

'And this is Colonel von Gratz.'

'Again, I know the name, sir, though I have not the honour of your acquaintance.'

'And Captain Markus,' Holmes finished.

'It is an unfeigned pleasure to meet you all, sirs,' said Norton. 'As indeed it would have been, even if the circumstances – oh, Irene!' And he broke off, his face lighting up with sheer joy as he looked beyond us to the doorway.

We turned, all of us at once, to see Mrs Norton standing there, her face mirroring the delight that shone from her husband's countenance.

'Godfrey! Are you well? They have not harmed you? Oh, Mr Holmes, gentlemen, how can I thank you properly?' Mrs Norton came into the room, and threw her arms around her husband. 'Mr Holmes, I know that you wanted me to wait in the carriage, but I could not. You are not too angry with me?'

'Not at all, madam. Indeed, I was just about to call you in and reunite you with Mr Norton.'

'How very touching!' came a sneering voice behind us.

'Karl!' cried Mrs Norton, looking beyond us.

We swung round, to see Karl von Ormstein standing

there, a revolver pointed at us. We had now relaxed our vigilance, thinking that we had been successful, and so we were totally unprepared for this latest shock. Both Holmes and Markus instinctively reached for their pistols, but Karl told them, 'I should not try it, gentlemen.'

'How on earth did you get here?' I asked him.

'I followed you, of course.'

'Ah!' said Holmes. 'I thought as much, but when nothing happened, I told myself that I was being fanciful. More to the point, what are you doing here? You have lost the game, you know.'

'Up to a point,' said Karl, with an air of reluctant agreement. 'I began to suspect that all was not well shortly after my meeting with the good doctor here. I examined the plate, just to be certain, and noticed that it was not the same one – there had been a minor blemish in the real plate. So I followed you, and paid Maurice a visit. We had a little – talk – in the course of which he told me his part in all this. I checked the plate you had given him, and saw at once that it was still not the genuine article! And so, Maurice having told me where Mr Norton was hidden, I took a special train, and got here only an hour or so after you did. Does that explain matters?'

'It still does not tell us why you are here,' Holmes pointed out. 'If you hope to seize the real plate, you will be disappointed, for it is broken into a hundred fragments.'

Karl nodded. 'An elementary precaution.'

'And, since your confederate Gottfried can no longer aspire to the throne –'

'Or, indeed, to anything else,' Karl put in. 'Once I had seen the second counterfeit plate, I paid Gottfried a little visit. Neither he nor Maurice will trouble the king again.'

'You scoundrel!' said von Gratz.

'Oh, come now! Were you not going to advise the king to have them arrested, banished, perhaps even executed? I have merely saved you the trouble,' said Karl.

Von Gratz said, 'There may yet be a way out of all this. The king has said that he wished to speak to you, and I am sure that some continuation of the old arrangement might be –'

'He wants to buy me off, you mean? As my father did?' Karl laughed. 'It is too late for that. And in any case, though the king might overlook my actions, the people and the council would never agree, not after the deaths of Gottfried and Maurice, little though either will be missed. And for good measure, I have already made some provision for my immediate future, for although both Gottfried and Maurice had houses and lands which I cannot hope to touch, they were both cautious men, and both had some considerable portable wealth, which I have appropriated since they cannot use it now.'

'So it is revenge and nothing more?' asked Holmes.

'Your grasp of the situation is admirable. And I think I shall start with you, Mr Holmes.'

As he spoke, Karl moved his revolver to point it directly at Holmes, and I clearly saw his finger tighten on the trigger. Suddenly, Godfrey Norton leapt forward, not towards Karl, but directly in front of Holmes, shielding him. At that instant Karl fired, and Norton gave a grunt and collapsed.

Several things happened at once. Holmes made to leap at Karl, but stumbled over the body of the unfortunate Norton. I pulled out my revolver, and von Gratz also found his. But Mrs Norton moved faster than any of us; she threw herself at Karl, who swung his pistol round and fired at her, once, twice, and she fell to the floor.

Then von Gratz and I fired at the same time. I shot Karl only once, but von Gratz emptied his pistol, firing again and again at Karl even as he too slumped to the floor.

'Watson? Are they badly injured?' Holmes asked me, as I rushed to the inert form of Mrs Norton.

A single glance told me all I needed to know. 'She is dead, Holmes.'

'And Norton?'

'I fear that he too is beyond my help.'

Holmes shook his head. 'We had just been introduced, yet he gave his life to save mine. Who could have thought it?'

Evidently not Norton himself, I thought, for there was a distinct look of surprise upon his face. What had prompted him to act in such a fashion, I asked myself. Had he thought of what he did, or was it merely some primitive instinct? Whatever the reason, it was indeed the act of a brave man.

'And Karl?' Holmes's voice recalled me to the present.

There was no need for me to examine Karl. His body, riddled with bullets and soaked with blood, told its own tale.

Holmes shook his head again. 'This is not the ending I had foreseen, Watson.'

'None of us could have predicted it,' said von Gratz. 'But at any rate, the king is safe, and so is all Bohemia.'

'That is something, I suppose,' said Holmes, as he turned away, a look of sadness on his face.

TWELVE

The two coffins lay side by side, their lids open. I glanced inside the first, to see the body of the unfortunate Godfrey Norton, a look of surprise still upon his face. Upon his chest were the broad ribbon and the star that marked the Grand Cordon of the Order of Saint Wenceslas. I gazed in silence for a moment. 'A brave man, Holmes.'

'Indeed he was.'

I stayed a moment longer, then moved to the other coffin, which bore the form of Mrs Norton. Again, the ribbon and star had been placed in the coffin, together with a single red rose. I shook my head sadly and then looked at Holmes, who was by my side.

He nodded to the attendant, and we walked slowly out, blinking in the spring sunshine, while behind us the lids were screwed down.

I said, 'You know, Holmes, so often I have said that "one thing puzzles me" about our cases.'

He smiled thinly. 'And what puzzles you about this one?'

'A small point, but it niggles. Why did Gottfried and Karl leave the safety of the castle and return to the city, where they were in much greater danger?'

'I have considered that myself, and I can only suppose that they feared a siege.'

'A siege?'

'It was always the one danger facing even the stoutest castle. If the king had sent a couple of regiments, invested the castle so that nobody could leave it alive –'

'Then they could not have used the photograph!'

Holmes nodded. 'The whole point of the photograph was that it must be available to show to the King of Scandinavia. Effectively locked inside the castle, safer than any bank strongroom, it would have been no threat. They might have plenty of food, and there is probably a well inside the castle grounds, but what of that, if they could not get out to use the photograph? The king did not plan a siege, of course, but Gottfried and Karl could not know that.'

'Indeed, I am surprised that none of us thought of surrounding the castle, Holmes. It would have saved a good deal of trouble!'

He gave me a sidelong glance. 'One cannot always think of the obvious, Watson. A pity, perhaps, as you say, for it might have saved the lives of the Nortons.' And he walked on in silence.

There were but the four of us at the grave side a little later that day; the king, von Gratz, Holmes and myself. When the brief ceremony was done, von Gratz saluted the graves, bowed to the king, and returned to the carriage.

'Mr Holmes?'

'A moment, Your Majesty. I shall perhaps make my own way back,' said Holmes, staring in silence at the graves.

The king nodded. 'Doctor?'

'Ah, yes, sire.' I followed the king, realizing that Holmes wanted a moment to himself.

I did not venture to break the silence, but the king evidently had that urge to talk which sometimes comes at such sad times. 'You saw the insignia of the Order?' he asked me. 'I placed them there myself.'

'A truly royal gesture, sire.'

He waved this away. 'The least I could do, Doctor. And, alas, the most! Would that it were otherwise.'

'It would have been much appreciated, Your Majesty.' Emboldened, I added, 'And I suspect that perhaps the red rose left in Mrs Norton's coffin would have been even more highly esteemed.'

The king stopped, turned, and stared at me. 'Red rose?' said he. 'I left no red rose.'